WITHDRAWN

SINGLETON'S LAW

SINGLETON'S LAW

Reginald Hill

G.K. Hall & Co. • Chivers Press
Thorndike, Maine USA   Bath, England

This Large Print edition is published by G.K. Hall & Co., USA
and by Chivers Press, England.

Published in 1997 in the U.S. by arrangement with
Chivers Press Ltd.

Published in 1997 in the U.K. by arrangement with
Severn House Publishers Ltd.

U.S. Hardcover   0-7838-8106-1   (Mystery Collection Edition)
U.K. Hardcover   0-7540-3040-7   (Chivers Large Print)
U.K. Softcover   0-7540-3041-5   (Camden Large Print)

British Library Cataloguing in Publication Data available

Library of Congress Cataloging in Publication Data

Hill, Reginald.
    [Albion! Albion!]
    Singleton's law / Reginald Hill.
      p.   cm.
    Previously published as: Albion! Albion! / Dick Morland [pseud.].
1974.
    ISBN 0-7838-8106-1 (lg. print : hc : alk. paper)
    1. Large type books. I. Title.
[PS6058.I448A72 1997]
823'.914—dc21   97-18507

Introduction

Youth is knowing that a decade is an eternity; *maturity* is knowing that the next ten years will pass in a flash; and *age* is not knowing if you'll make it to the weekend.

I must have been pretty young when I wrote SINGLETON'S LAW under the original title of ALBION! ALBION! I saw no problem whatever in setting the book in the nineties with many back references to radical changes in the political structure of the United Kingdom during the eighties. Now my fictional future can be set alongside a real past and the world can judge what a lousy prophet I was.

On the other hand I have always preferred parable to prophecy, and I reckon very little to either unless contained in a cracking good story. Many people were kind enough to describe AL-BION! ALBION! in these terms back in the seventies. I hope my new readers will feel the same.

Reginald Hill
February 1997

I behold London, a Human awful wonder of
   God.
He says: "Return, Albion, return! I give myself
   for thee.
My Streets are my Ideas of Imagination.
Awake Albion, awake! and let us awake up
   together.

Jerusalem: WILLIAM BLAKE

Extract from Preamble to Fifth Series of Richard M. Nixon Lectures in Modern History given annually at Yale University

Knowledge must precede understanding, and during the next few weeks I shall spend much time describing rather than analysing the state of this unhappy country. I have gathered together a body of material — film, tape, documents, letters — some of which you may find distasteful but all of which I believe to be of prime importance. I should like at this stage to offer my thanks to the many individuals and groups who have helped in its compilation — the President and the relevant White House departments, the library of Congress, the staff of the Film and Tape Archives Section of the Institute of Contemporary Studies, the C.I.A. . . . .

Chapter 1

Even sunsets become boring after three hours. Whitey Singleton pressed the button which let him hear what the intense young man above his head was saying to the blousy blonde with the schismatic tits ". . . a pair of reechy kisses, or paddling in your neck with his damn'd fingers . . ."

He groaned. Sixty thousand feet over Asia, who needs a 1920's Hamlet? Another button gave him the Japanese historical drama. A kimono'd stewardess arriving with his drink smiled at him approvingly, and he waited till she had disappeared along the blue carpeted aisle before switching off.

He took a magazine from the rack in front of him and groaned again when he saw it was last week's *Nuspic*.

He knew the articles almost by heart. The World Money Crisis. The ingenious solution of it by persons yet unknown who had dug a hundred foot tunnel into the vaults of a Los Angeles bank and removed a million dollars. The usual attack on the E.E.C.

And there as always in the centre spread was his own name, alongside the solemn photo and above the punchy prose.

The picture never changed. It was five years old now, taken when he first joined the paper shortly after settling in the States. He glanced at himself in the glass port. It was like Dorian Gray in reverse. The thought raised a smile which made him look younger but still not very like the solemn twenty-five year old of the photo. *He* reminded Whitey of someone else. Yes, that was it. Hamlet laying down the law to his poor old mother. Not the features, just the expression. Preachy righteousness.

Whitey yawned widely, his normal reflex in face of the disquieting, whether mental or physical. So he preached a bit. At least that way things got said and heard. And he kept a balance. The photo lied, he assured himself; which wasn't such a bad thing. There were many advantages for a journalist in anonymity.

He took a pad from his pocket and began to sketch some preliminary notes for his first piece on the Sudanese war. His critics might accuse him of pre-judging the situation, but two hours after landing he would be sending his first report home, so time was of the essence.

He glanced through the port. The plane was just overflying another cloud shelf and there, not quite dead ahead and just visible from his side of the aisle, was the orb of the sun which their speed had kept balanced on the horizon ever since leaving Tokyo. He tried to whip up some enthusiasm in himself for either the beauties of nature or the marvels of technology. It wasn't good for a creative journalist to become desensitized. But it was hard work.

His glass he noticed with surprise was empty. Some Nipponese version of whisky, perhaps, so volatile that if you didn't get it down in ten seconds, it just evaporated. He rang the bell for the stewardess.

A few seats ahead of him a bulky man with an unhealthily pale face stood up and started down the aisle, followed by a slim girl who Whitey would have guessed to be a Westerner but whose face was made up to an almost Oriental smoothness of complexion and feature. Only the hydrangea-blue eyes weren't quite right. He watched her go by without interest. Two weeks on a story in Tokyo had whet his appetite for more expressive beauties.

He returned to his notes. Perhaps he was in fact pre-judging the situation. But hell! you didn't have to be on the spot to know what was right and what was wrong. All you needed to find out for yourself was which was winning. Usually there was little doubt of that, either.

He rang the service bell again impatiently. A stewardess appeared bearing a laden coffee tray high in front of her face, like an icon in procession. The uneasiness caused by a sense of his own cynicism made him uncharacteristically rude. As she passed without slowing, he grasped her kimono, bringing her to a halt which almost toppled the coffee pot. She looked down at him, expressionless except for the eyes whose dusty blue was momentarily polished by a bright fury.

"One moment, sir," she lisped and continued on her way.

He watched her move swiftly down the aisle and ring for admittance to the flight-deck. She glanced back as she waited for the security scrutiny to take place and the door to be opened. For a moment their gazes locked.

Hydrangea-blue eyes, thought Whitey. Unusual. But not impossible.

But even as he reassured himself, he knew that this was the girl who a few minutes earlier had walked past him in the direction of the toilets. And the galley.

He half rose, uncertain what he was going to do. The unhealthy fat man loomed over him and pushed him gently back into his seat.

"Watch the pretty picture," he said, snapping the viewing switch back on.

Claudius, very smart in an admiral's uniform, was speaking. 'Hamlet, this deed, for thine especial safety — which we do tender, as we dearly grieve for that which thou hast done — must send thee hence with fiery quickness . . .'

Out of Hamlet's mouth there seemed to issue the printed words *fasten your seatbelts*. There was a slight murmur of surprise and activity as the passengers complied except for two men who rose from different parts of the plane, hurried forward and with the fat man disappeared through the unlocked door of the flight-deck.

A few minutes later Whitey, imprisoned like

12

the rest of the passengers in the strong clasp of his seat belt, noticed that the sun, though still balanced on the horizon's rim, seemed to have rolled through about forty degrees to its left, and he knew for certain then that the aeroplane's destination was no longer Khartoum. He leaned back in his seat, stared unseeingly at a plain in Denmark on which Hamlet wearing a straw boater stood talking to a Norwegian captain, and began to yawn convulsively.

It was a highly efficient hi-jack. Many of the passengers did not even suspect anything was wrong till arrival time came and passed. A reassuring female voice then explained over the speaker system that there had been a slight change of plan, inconvenience was regretted but nobody need worry. The stewardesses had been instructed to supply the passengers' drinking and eating needs and of course there would be no charge.

Whitey almost smiled at this, but as he began to suspect where the plane was headed, he got further and further away from a smiling mood. Every international reporter has places in the world where he is unwelcome. Usually this simply means he will not be allowed to enter the country. But sometimes it means that, having got in, he will find it almost impossible to leave.

And when two hours later the great strato-jet finally settled on the runway and rolled majestically along between rows of fire-tenders, ambulances and security-guards, Whitey knew he had come back to the last place on earth he would have wished to be.

For a while a kind of pessimistic vanity made him fear that the whole thing might have been arranged for his special benefit. On the last occasion he had been in this state, he had narrowly escaped with his life and ever since then he had peppered its rulers with advice, accusation and abuse, from all corners of the globe. They would like him back, he was certain. But he was surely not all that important. Worth a knife in the back, some day, perhaps, but not a public kidnapping. In any case, he had booked his seat on this plane at the airport only an hour before departure.

Gradually he relaxed. Nothing happened for half-an-hour. He presumed some kind of negotiations were going on, and finally an open jeep drew up alongside the plane, followed by a truck out of which clambered four armed guards in tight fitting red uniform. Two of them were accompanied by very nasty-looking dogs, but when the hi-jackers climbed down from the plane, their greeting seemed friendly enough and they were driven off in the jeep without incident.

Next a tall stooping man in shirt-sleeves wearily boarded the plane.

"Preds," he said, giving the local greeting accompanied by the clenched fist salute with thumb upraised. The man then addressed the passengers, with one of the stewardesses interpreting for those who did not speak the language.

The plane would be taking off for its original destination after being refuelled and checked. Meanwhile the passengers were invited to step down and make use of the airport reception and catering facilities.

Whitey had no desire to leave the plane, but everybody else was moving and the last thing he wanted to be was conspicuous. No. The second last thing. The last thing was dead.

He walked in the middle of the caravan of passengers which wound its way to the huge reception area and once inside he headed straight for the toilets and locked himself in a cubicle. It was undignified but dignity was an expensive commodity if it left you short of life. These were people with a tradition of casual violence. The boot could go in so quickly that the only protection you could look for from an American passport was to hold it over your crotch.

He sat for nearly three hours, listening to announcements over the speakers. From time to time when he was sure the place was empty, he changed cubicles so that nobody could remark on the length of time any particular door was locked.

Finally the announcement came. The plane was ready for departure. Would passengers please assemble at gate number seven? He counted up to thirty, pulled the plug and stepped out.

A man was washing his hands at one of the row of brilliant white basins which bounced the

15

harsh strip-lighting back against the tiled ceiling. He was tall, stooping, in his shirtsleeves.

"No hurry, Mr. Singleton," he said wearily.

Whitey headed for the door which opened before he could reach it. Two men stepped in wearing the red uniform he had seen by the plane. The tight fitting trousers made their thick-soled brown boots seem huge.

" 'Preds," said one of them.

" 'Preds," answered the stooping man, drying his hands in a warm-air jet.

"This reffer?"

"This is Mr. Singleton."

"Reffing bastard," said the man and swung a flailing right hook which Whitey saw coming so far off that he even had time to resurrect a possible counter-move from his teenage judo training as he ducked beneath the blow. But his assailant's less talkative companion offered no such notice of intent. The metal-tipped boot caught him just below the knee and he shrieked in agony as he fell. *Keep on your feet* was the only bit of teenage fighting lore that came to him now and he dragged himself half upright against one of the wash-basins, gripping the taps for support. A fist thudded into the small of his back and he shrieked again, but hung on. In the mirror he could see his attackers clearly, or as clearly as his tear-filled eyes would permit. The talking man moved forward and he tensed himself for another blow, but it didn't come. Instead the man turned on the hot tap and a gush of near boiling water

16

broke over his right hand. He let go and fell back.

Now the blows came fast, mainly from the boots though an occasional punch was thrown if his writhings brought his head within striking distance. In the background the drone of the hot-air drier went on and on, mingling with and absorbing all other noises till it seemed to enter his head and become the only functioning part of his consciousness.

Then it stopped, and he thought he must be dead.

"That's time," said the stooping man's voice. "Take him out."

Ten minutes later he came to in the back of a moving van which smelt as if it had been used for carrying dogs. The ear which wasn't bleeding caught the noise of a jet taking off and he wondered if it was his flight. He managed to push himself off the ground till his face was level with the metal grille which covered the rear window.

There was no hope of glimpsing the departing plane but with the eye that wasn't closed, he saw the huge road sign which they were rapidly leaving behind them.

It read HEATHROW AIRPORT. ALL TRAFFIC SLOW.

Nixon Lectures : Fifth Series

Extract from preamble

The rise of the Four Clubs is my theme. I shall from time to time glance at the Scottish Two Club system and at those parts of Wales and the West Country which still deny allegiance to any Club; but England is my main concern.

Someone once said that language is history in the making and in support of this I should like to draw your attention to the document folder in the rack before you.

Documentary Material

1 **(a)** Extracts from MIDDLETON'S *New International Dictionary*; British Supplement (1994)

blest, int. Form of greeting in mid-English territory governed by Wanderers Club (contr. of *blue is best* referring to Club colour; sometimes falsely derived from *be blessed*). Note also **preds** (S.E. form, contr. of *up the reds!*), **greening** (N.E. form, corruption of *greeting*), and **yellow** (N.W. form, corruption of *hello!*).

glib, a. & n. Homo-sexual, particularly a member of a transvestite group, frequently violent (contr. of *gay liberation,* defunct protest group of sixties and seventies).

nonleague, a. Below standard; finished; knackered.

norm, n. Non-active member of Four Clubs society.

plite, int. Farewell (contr. of *play it tight,* in common use throughout England. See also **smatch,** int., contr. of *see you at the match*).

reffer, n. Blackguard, scoundrel (term of great abuse; fr. referee, arbiter in old football competitions. Also exists as v. **reff,** commonly used with **off** with strength of *fuck off!* Also part.-ing).

relegate, v.t. Demote (often euphem. for beat unconscious, murder).

striker, n. active member of the main security force of one of the Four Clubs, usually known as the First Team. But also used for any member of the disciplinary cadre of a Supporters' (q.v.) Club. (Fr. obs. sport. slang, one whose purpose in the game of football was to score goals).

supporter, n. Member of the myriad clubs formed to pledge support to the Management of one of the Four Clubs. (N.B. These Supporters' Clubs' range from mere social centres to hotbeds of fanatical extremism, especially in the universities).

yuss, v.t. Use superior strength to enforce one's will; (*yussing,* though nowhere defined in writing, is at the basis of Four Club law; a Supporter may do what he has the power to to do. Fr. L. *ius virium,* the law of force. See Mr. Justice Lauriston's summing up *Rex v. Woodcock and others,* March 1985).

Chapter 2

The Governor of Wormwood Scrubs was not pleased by Whitey's arrival in his office.

"What you want me to do with this reffer?" he demanded.

"Just look after him till I see the Manager," said the stooping man persuasively.

"He's so important?"

"I think it. He's Singleton. You remember?"

"Singleton? Oh yes. *That* Singleton."

Whitey, supported between the two large men, revived slightly at the mention of his name.

"I demand to see the American Consul," he said. At least those were the words that formed in his mind, but what sounds emerged from his swollen and split lips he could not tell.

"All right," said the Governor, capitulating suddenly. "Chuck him in. But he's your ball, Sheldrake."

From somewhere inside the building came a long shriek, cut off suddenly. Sheldrake looked enquiringly at the Governor who shrugged.

"The girl," he said. "Some of the team are having a bit of fun."

"The reffing idiots!" protested Sheldrake. "We might want her."

"Up to you," said the Governor. "There's six

of them. You want to yuss it?"

Sheldrake glanced at his two henchmen who looked back at him neutrally.

"No," he said. "It's too late anyway. But no one touches this one or I'll yuss it with half a dozen strikers. OK?"

"By the look of him, you'd need a glass to find anywhere that hasn't been done over already," said the Governor. "Take him down. We're a bit full, but we'll squeeze him in somewhere. You want a sponge for him or is he to be let fester?"

Sheldrake thought a moment, then nodded.

"All right. Call the quack. I'd like him to be taking notice when the Man sees him. The girl too."

"Her? She won't need a doctor, just a long rest."

The men laughed together knowingly and the sound went with Whitey into the depths of the prison, where it was lost in other clanging, metallic noises, voices shouting, all amplified and dehumanized by the great shaft of dead space which fell through the building's centre. For what might have been an hour, even two, he lay on the floor of a cell before he was lifted up once more and carried to a small surgery. Here a middle-aged doctor probed and prodded for a while, then set to work. A gash on his brow needed eight stitches, another on his left arm six. Two teeth had been broken and one of these was so loose that it would need a dentist's attention. His ribs were strapped and his numerous other

21

gashes and bruises were washed and dressed. When it was over, he felt a great deal better, mainly through relief at the relatively minor nature of the damage. Sheldrake's desire to keep him in some kind of trim for further treatment must have made him instruct his men to aim at maximum pain but minimum damage.

The Doctor wanted to keep him in the hospital ward, but the two prison officers who had taken over from Sheldrake's thugs demurred.

"He'll be all right, won't you, old son?" said one of them, clamping his arm round Whitey's shoulders in an apparently friendly gesture which made him wince with pain.

"Of course he will," said the other. "This is Whitey Singleton, doc. One of nature's winners, is Whitey."

Laughing (it seemed a popular pastime here), they took him out and amused themselves by pushing him from one to the other as they walked down the long narrow corridor which led to the cells. At first in the best Anglo-Stoic tradition he tried not to show his pain but after a while the effort did not seem worth the doubtful moral satisfaction.

"Did that hurt?" asked one of them at the first groan. "I'm sorry, mate. Hey, George, watch what you're doing. Whitey's hurt and you know we haven't got to hurt him."

"True," said George. "You've got real supporters somewhere, Whitey. Powerful friends ready to yuss things if anyone harms you."

"Not that a few more bruises would really be noticed, would they?"

"No they wouldn't," said George reflectively. "But we'd better be careful. Tell you what we could do, though. We can't be responsible for what the prisoners do to each other, can we? We could put him in with one of those Wanderers wankers."

They started laughing again and a couple of minutes later Whitey was thrust into a cell with such force that he fell flat on his face and felt strong reminder impulses go rushing out to his many wounds.

When he looked up, he saw the cell was already occupied. A man in prison clothes crouched in a defensive position against the furthermost wall. He looked as if he too had received a beating fairly recently, but there was nothing cringing about his stance. The grey eyes in the long angular face were wary, but that was all.

There was someone else here too. On the lower of the two bunks lay a slight figure paying no attention whatsoever to proceedings. With a shock Whitey realized it was a woman. One long white leg trailed on the floor, the other was crooked across the rough grey blankets.

"Mr. Chaucer sir," said George from the doorway. "Another one to keep you company. Let me introduce you. This is Mr. Chaucer, a very important person. Assistant Manager with Wanderers, believe it or not. And this, Mr. Chaucer, is someone you may remember. Mr. Singleton.

No? Mr. *Whitey* Singleton. There, I knew you'd remember. See how we look after our guests!"

"Reff off," said Chaucer.

"Naughty," reproved George. "Be good now. Smatch!"

The door clanged shut. As quickly as he could Whitey started to rise to his feet, never taking his eyes off the man. He felt himself yawning widely. Perhaps this gave an impression of sang froid as the other spoke first.

"Is it right? You're Singleton?"

"Yes." It still hurt him to speak.

"Why've they put you in here with me?"

"I think they hope you'll attack me."

Chaucer thought a moment.

"That's fair. I might do," he said. "But what's stopping them?"

"Any more treatment for me's been yussed for them."

Chaucer laughed. Whitey began to doubt whether he would ever hear laughter again without a tremor of fear.

"They left it late, didn't they?" said Chaucer staring pointedly at Whitey's array of dressings. The figure on the lower bunk stirred and for the first time Whitey took his eyes off Chaucer.

The woman was trying to sit up, pulling her torn dress tightly round her. It was this dress that Whitey recognized first. Crushed, ripped and soiled, it was still recognizable as a kimono. Old gold with a delicate flower pattern, the uniform of Tokyo Airlines.

24

The woman herself took a second longer. The hair was dishevelled and fell raggedly over a face from which the smooth Oriental make-up had been removed by tears and bruises. But as on the plane, the hydrangea eyes were the giveaway. It was the girl hi-jacker.

He moved towards her and was startled by the fear and hate which showed in her face as she retreated into the bunk recess like a frightened animal in a cave.

"Are you all right?" he asked.

She didn't answer. He didn't blame her. It was a stupid question.

"Leave the stupid bitch alone," said Chaucer. "I want to talk to you."

Reluctantly Whitey turned away. Chaucer had seated himself on the one chair the room possessed, which was a comforting sign. In his present state, Whitey knew he was a push-over, but even so, no one was going to attack him from a sitting position.

"What made you come back?" asked Chaucer.

"She did," said Whitey, jerking his head towards the girl and wishing he hadn't.

"What?"

"I was on the flight she hi-jacked."

"Oh. That's how she got here, was it?" Chaucer shrugged indifferently. "She'd have been better off stopping where she was, that's certain. What are they going to do with you?"

"I don't know. I heard them mention the Manager."

"Oh, he'll want to see you right enough, I reckon," said Chaucer grimly. "Mine too. You're not exactly a much-loved man, Singleton."

"No."

Chaucer stood up suddenly and Whitey backed away.

"Never fear," said the man reaching under the pillow of the upper bunk for a packet of cigarettes. "I won't touch you. Nothing I could do would be a shadow of what you've got coming."

"You seem to have taken a bit yourself," said Whitey with an attempt at bravado.

The man touched his bruised face, his fingers running down a line of scratches which seemed the most recent adornment.

"Nothing but a bit of exercise," he said lightly. "I've got a transfer value if I'm kept in trim."

Whitey recognized the attempt at self reassurance but decided it would be wiser not to comment. Suddenly the woman spoke.

"I've been raped seven times," she said in a quick low voice.

"You think that's some kind of record?" said Chaucer.

Whitey glared angrily at him and sat down on the edge of the bunk. He was remembering Sheldrake and the Governor's brief reference to the girl.

"Did they take you to the doctor?" he asked.

"Yes."

"Didn't he give you something?"

"Yes. A sedative. Then they put me in here."

26

She was crying now. It can't have been a very efficient sedative, thought Whitey. But the tears might relax her.

"It's OK, it's OK," he said helplessly. "Try to sleep. Try to get some rest. You're with friends."

"In here?" she screamed suddenly. "Friends? Like him?" She pushed by Whitey and stood upright, facing Chaucer who smiled at her and gently touched the scratches on his face.

"You mean, he's one of . . ." began Whitey.

"What's the odds?" demanded Chaucer. "You heard her. Six of them. So why not one of me? I've been in here a month. Just you wait, Singleton. Not that you'll have the strength after a month."

Whitey flung a round-arm right at him. He didn't bother to duck but caught the strengthless blow contemptuously in the palm of his left hand.

"Play it tight, lad," he said. "I'm not averse to sorting you out if that's what you want. Only I don't see why I should do these reffers' work for them."

"You didn't mind with her," said Whitey bitterly, subsiding on to the bunk.

"That's different. I get no kicks out of doing a man over, but I like my home comforts. Any road, why're you so snarled about her? It's her fault you're here. I shouldn't feel obligated in your shoes."

Whitey recognized the logic in this. Certainly if it had been the unhealthy looking male hijacker in the cell with him, he doubted if he'd

27

have had much sympathy to spare. Though in a way his indignation on the girl's behalf was merely selfish in that it took his mind off his own predicament. Most human sympathy and generosity of spirit sprang from a kind of delight in recognizing that someone else was lower down on the scale of suffering, he thought gloomily.

"Right. Boy scout time over," said Chaucer. "You've had a long hard day. Get some rest while you can."

"What time is it?" asked Whitey, surprised by this sudden solicitude.

"God knows. One, two o'clock in the morning? They don't give you clocks."

Whitey ran his mind back over the events of the day. Yes, it must be at least midnight, probably much later.

"How shall we manage?" he yawned, indicating the two bunks.

"You two take them," said Chaucer magnanimously. "The chair'll do me. Get some rest."

The girl who seemed to have relapsed into a near-catatonic state, revived at the discussion of sleeping arrangements.

"No," she said. What she was refusing Whitey could not quite make out. But what she feared was plain enough.

"It's all right," said Chaucer. "Don't worry, love. He's not going to bother you and I've had enough. You didn't exactly make me welcome, did you?"

"I'll kill you," said the girl flatly.

"Maybe. Look, you get up aloft if you're worried. That way, if I did come looking for comfort, I'd be bound to wake up young Lochinvar here."

The girl said no more but clambered into the upper bunk while Whitey stretched out below. The blankets still held her body-warmth and above him the mattress creaked as she shifted in search of ease. What had been the motive for the hi-jacking? he wondered. And why had she received such brutal treatment in the country of her choice?

He lacked data on which to hypothesize. In any case his own troubles were demanding the full attention of his mind. He doubted if he could sleep.

"Ready?" said Chaucer reaching up to the unguarded bulb in the ceiling. "Smatch."

He gave it a half twist and the cell went dark.

"Smatch," said Whitey, wondering why this hard man from the North was suddenly overflowing with the milk of human kindness.

Again there could be no answer. But the small break from the contemplation of his own dismal prospects gave his great fatigue the chance it needed. Quickly it slid in, occupied every inch of his body and mind.

And within seconds he was asleep.

Documentary Material

3 (g) Extract from the report of the Football League's committee of investigation into the causes and control of hooliganism in football grounds. May 1981

It can be seen that the situation has changed radically since our last report. Then our concern was, in part at least, that growing hooliganism was driving supporters away from football. But now it is the tremendous rise in gate numbers, (doubled and even trebled in the past five years), that helps cause trouble. Enthusiasm has never been greater. But nor has partisanship. This is why we have so strongly urged the improvement of the purely physical measures of crowd control. If the outer perimeters of stadia are strengthened and patrolled, the number in the ground can be restricted to the legal maximum. Internal segregation of opposing supporters into clearly marked and strongly fenced pens will cut down fighting on the terraces. And the introduction round the pitch of double crash barriers, high close-mesh wire fencing (lightly electrified, if necessary) and concrete moats will prevent trespass on the playing area.

But of course these measures are nothing unless the police and judiciary are given powers to deal much more harshly with offenders . . .

Chapter 3

Whitey awoke.

There were burglars downstairs.

No, he recalled. There is no downstairs here. And all the burglars are locked up.

But the certainty of intrusion remained.

His eyes were winning their battle against the dark, and the cell's shape and furniture were starting to emerge in gradations of grey. Not that there was much to see. A blank wall. A small table. A chair.

There was nobody sitting on the chair.

Cold with anger, Whitey rolled stealthily out of his bunk. If Chaucer was not visible, there was only one place he could be.

Gently raising the chair as a weapon, he peered into the upper bunk.

The girl had been crying before she fell asleep and her cheeks were still wet. But she slept peacefully now and was alone.

Whitey replaced the chair. As his anger melted, his aches and pains came hurrying back, offended that he had forgotten them. But he still ignored them, concentrating his mind on the problem before him. It could have only one solution, so absurdly simple that he hardly dared test it.

He crossed to the door, took the best grip he

could on its almost smooth surface, and pulled.

It swung easily open.

The darkness and the silence that lay outside made the little grey cube of the cell seem warm and cosy. If he stepped back inside, and closed the door, and pulled the blankets over his head, and went to sleep . . . he would be woken up in the morning, questioned, beaten, and ultimately taken out into some sunless yard and put to death.

The motion is carried unanimously, he said to himself and began to close the door behind him.

"What's happening?" asked the girl.

Her voice was pitched low but in this silence it seemed to resound like a bell. For a moment he thought of keeping going, but there was no way of locking the door behind him and she would surely follow. Her future scarcely seemed more rosy than his own. He made his way back to the bunk. She was sitting on the edge, her legs dangling.

"Chaucer's gone," he said. "The door's open. Don't ask me what it means."

"And you were going too?"

"Why not?" he asked with a defensive shrug.

"I'm coming too," she said, pushing herself forward preparatory to descent. Automatically he raised his arms to assist her. She froze.

"Lady," he said wearily. "You flatter yourself."

"I didn't look my best before, either," she retorted, but completed the drop, accepting the support of his hands.

At the door he felt her react as he had done to the brooding darkness outside.

"What's happening?" she whispered.

"God knows," he said. "I reckon there's been some kind of rescue attempt made for Chaucer. We'll just have to try to tack on to the tail-end of it. Give me your hand."

This time there was no hesitation about contact. Curious, thought Whitey as the slender rather chilly fingers grasped his tightly. She accepts as kindness what is purest self-interest. I'd rather she were still asleep, but awake, she's better close by me than wandering around by herself.

"Come on," he whispered.

The darkness out here was even more reluctant to unveil its mysteries than that in the cell. But bitter experience leaves traces in the mind that no amount of comfort can expunge, and Whitey found himself moving ahead with growing confidence. His companion sensed it.

"You know your way around," she commented.

"You never forget places where you've been happy," answered Whitey. "No talking from now on in. OK?"

He had spent only a few weeks here before being shifted to the 'hulks', the infamous string of prison ships moored from Woolwich to Rotherhither. A curious spin-off of the breakdown of law had been a rapidly growing pressure on prison space. Fewer laws seemed to equal more prisoners. It was an equation Whitey viewed with some affection. Without it, the move to Woolwich and the chance of escape might never have come. He had not had the kind of support or organization behind him which could arrange a rescue such as Chaucer's.

If it were a rescue. Perhaps Chaucer had merely been taken out for questioning. Or execution. And the open door was a sadistic joke, a lure to draw him into an escape attempt. But against this, he recalled Chaucer's surprising magnanimity in permitting the girl and himself to have the bunks. He must have known his supporters were planning a break-out that night and wanted his cell-mates out of the way. Whitey felt an illogical resentment that the man had not offered to take him along, but pushed so irrelevant an emotion to the back of his mind. All that mattered about the escape was the amount of time that had passed since Chaucer's departure. Checks were made at regular intervals, he remembered. An hour, two hours, he forgot the exact details, which in any case, might have changed since his time. But if Chaucer had been gone upwards of an hour, then discovery must be imminent.

The thought filled him with panic and he increased his pace for a couple of strides till reason got control once more. His eyes had grown more used to the blackness and a change in its intensity plus his own revived memories told him he was approaching the metal stairway which descended

34

a dozen steps into the old recreation centre. Prisoners' recreation was a concept long discarded, partly through pressures on space but mainly because the philosophy on which it was based had been discredited. The area was used for other things now — accommodation, interrogation — but the use which concerned Whitey most was that it contained the warders' night duty room.

The gate at the top of the stairs was unlocked, confirming that this was the route Chaucer had taken. He and his supporters were not wasting time locking up behind them.

He broke the silence for the first time in several minutes and murmured, "stairs", to the girl, pulling her behind him and resting her hand on his shoulder. The other hand sought his other shoulder and she came up close behind, leaning into his back. He winced at the pain this caused.

There was one stair less than he remembered and the jarring this gave his leg was almost as bad as missing a step. The sudden breaking of the rhythm they had set up during the descent unbalanced the girl and she fell forward against him. The pain this time made the earlier twinges a pleasant memory. He staggered forward a few paces with his companion clinging at his waist. Then the ground fell away under his feet and he crashed full length, remembering as he did so that the miscounted step was not a stair-tread, but a concrete step-down a yard from the foot of the stairs.

As his chest struck the ground he let out a cry of pain. The girl, prostrate over his legs, dug him in the back with what he took to be a reprimanding blow. *Her* ribs weren't broken, he thought indignantly. She poked him again; this time he began to push himself upright preparatory to dealing with her; then he saw what she must have seen already.

Light. A thin golden line in the wash of grey. As he stared at it, it grew, thickened, ran out across the concrete floor on which he lay.

A door was slowly opening.

He tried to struggle to his feet but the girl seemed to be transfixed and he could not shake her weight from his legs. In any case there would scarcely have been time to retreat up the stairs before whoever was coming out appeared at the door. He managed to reach a kneeling position and waited. A posture of supplication seemed not unfitting though he doubted whether it would have any effect.

The person coming from the warders' room was taking his time. And the first sign of him was odd. A hand came round the door, grasping the jamb and apparently trying to pull it further open. And the hand was only a few inches from the floor.

Now the girl seemed to regain her strength and pushed herself upright. Whitey followed suit and together they approached the room. As they did so the hand made a last convulsive effort and the door rolled back another foot. Whitey stepped inside and found himself looking down at George.

Whether George recognized him or not, it was hard to say. Whether Whitey hoped he did was just as hard. Certainly the warder's eyes were open and apparently focused. Blood ran down the side of his head from a wide gash along the top of his skull. But this was not the man's significant wound. His tunic was open and out of a hole in his chest pumped spurt after spurt of blood.

By the far wall of the room lay another warder, eyes open, too still to be anything but dead. George's route along the floor towards the door was clearly marked in thick brown stains. It passed a telephone which had been wrenched from the wall.

The girl pushed by him and looked round the room, poker-faced.

"What happened?" was all she said.

"God knows. I'd say that Chaucer's strikers got in here, knocked them senseless, then . . ."

". . . killed them," completed the girl. "They didn't do such a good job on him, did they?"

She glanced at George and moved to the other man, kneeling down by his body.

For a second Whitey thought this was merely vain solicitude.

"He's dead," he said.

"I know it," she replied, standing up with the warder's truncheon in her hand. "But not long. We must be pretty close behind Chaucer. Let's move."

She made for the door.

"Wait a moment," Whitey protested looking down at George who still crouched spaniel-like at his feet.

"For Godsake," she said. "We've got to move fast. We might just be able to walk out behind them, especially if they've been as thorough as this all the way in."

She indicated the room with a delicate gesture.

"What about *him?*" asked Whitey pointing at George.

"What about him?" she asked, her features set once more. "You forget, I've met both these gentlemen already."

George seemed to react to something in her tone. He made a great effort to pull himself upright, the blood pumped forth with increased force, he opened his mouth to speak, then he died.

"There you are," said the girl. "Like I said, no problem. Come on."

Abandoning caution now, they moved as fast as the darkness would permit them, following what Whitey guessed would be Chaucer's exit route. They met three more dead warders on the way. The rescue party's technique had been comparatively simple. After the initial entry of the building, they had murdered anyone they met and used the keys so obtained to open up the next sector. It was the plan either of a lunatic or of someone who knew just how casual and disorganized the prison's security system had become. In either case, it looked as if it was going to work.

They caught their first glimpse of Chaucer and his men as they stepped out into the main entrance yard. The paleness of dawn was already in the sky and after the oppressing blackness inside, the yard seemed almost floodlit by the starlight flickering fitfully through the scudding clouds. Moving along the base of the main wall to their left three or four men were visible for a couple of seconds before the shadows took them. They must have come in over the wall — once again the obvious, straightforward thing to do.

"Let's hope they're as generous with ladders as they have been with open doors," Whitey murmured to the girl.

"What?"

"If they pull their little bits of rope up behind them, we might as well go back to our cell."

She reflected on this for a moment.

"That's all right," she said finally. "If they show any sign of doing that, we'll let out a yell. They'll think they've been spotted and after that no-one's going to hang around to pull up a ladder. Come on."

Ingenious, thought Whitey, then seized the girl violently from behind as she made to step out of the doorway. Her slim body twisted convulsively in his arms but she did not cry out.

"Look!" he hissed urgently. "By the main gate!"

"I can't see anything."

"No. He's gone. But someone moved. He must have gone through the wicket door."

"Who? One of Chaucer's men?"

"Don't be stupid."

No. Not one of Chaucer's men. But someone watching. It *was* the plan of a lunatic. It failed because it relied on killing people and with every warder they killed, they broke part of the security circuit. Once the first body was discovered you could either set every alarm in the place going, or take a walk around the perimeter and spot where they were going to come out. With desperate men, probably armed, it would be much better to get them in your sights before making a challenge. Which meant that sitting at the other side of the wall there would be a little posse, calmly waiting for the kill.

That it would be a kill, Whitey was sure. With their colleagues lying murdered inside, it was going to take more than a few orders to stop the ambush party from massacring the escapers. And it was doubtful whether anyone would care to give such orders anyway.

"Wait here," he commanded the girl.

"Why? What . . ."

He pushed her to one side and set off at a painful trot across the yard. Even if there had been more than one watcher within, it didn't matter. A shot was the only thing that could stop him and a shot would arouse everybody.

He was almost at the east wall before he saw

them. Three men were crouched on top of it, another two were climbing up knotted ropes. As he watched two of the men on top dropped out of sight down the far side. The outside. The free side.

Suppose he were wrong, thought Whitey. Suppose he had been mistaken and there was no ambush out there, nothing except freedom.

The other two men had reached the top. He assumed that the man in the middle was Chaucer. It seemed to fit — two going on ahead to prepare the way, another two coming behind to guard the rear. Any moment now he too was going to disappear over the wall.

What do I care about him anyway? thought Whitey.

And stepping from the shadows he shouted between funnelled hands, "Chaucer! don't go over the wall! They're waiting for you!"

The three men froze. Whitey could almost feel the shock and fear which must have run through their bodies at his voice. Then they did exactly what the girl had forecast they would do if challenged. They took off.

Well, I tried, thought Whitey as they disappeared. Time I started thinking of myself.

He turned away from the wall, a shape detached itself from the blackness just below the parapet, slid with hand-scorching speed down a rope, dropping the last ten feet and flinging itself forward like a projectile which did not pause till it bore Whitey to the ground.

"Right, you bastard!" said Chaucer. "I want . . ."

But what he wanted was never spoken. A fusillade of shots cracked out on the other side of the wall. They could hear quite clearly lead striking stone. There was a confusion of shouts.

As though at a command, Chaucer and Whitey started running, Whitey slightly in the lead, Chaucer following. They were heading towards the main gate which seemed stupid. The men outside would be pouring through there at any moment as soon as they realized they hadn't got Chaucer. But it was where he'd left the girl and he had to go back.

My trouble is I think I'm responsible for everybody, he told himself bitterly.

The shooting was continuing sporadically which was good. They couldn't start examining bodies till everyone was dead.

The main gate was in sight and someone was moving in front of it. So he had been right — someone had remained and they would have no qualms at all about shooting now.

"We've had it," he gasped to Chaucer.

Now the guard on the gate was moving to intercept them. Or get them in range. And he was shouting now.

"For Christ's sake!" yelled the girl. "Where are you going?"

Whitey stopped and Chaucer cannoned into him.

42

"I thought you were the guard," Whitey said absurdly.

"No. That's the guard." She pointed at a crumpled shape on the flag stones by the gate. "He came out to take a look at you and set off to stalk you with his little gun. Fortunately . . ."

She thrust her stolen baton obscenely into the air.

"Is he dead?" asked Whitey incredulously.

"God knows. But those warders inside are. We've got to go."

"Go? Where?"

"Out through the gate, of course. I have keys."

Something happened which Whitey could not quite place at once. Then he realized. The firing had stopped.

"Come on!" he said.

They spoke no more but charged across the yard to the gate. The girl had already fitted the key into the lock. It turned easily and within seconds they were outside and running madly past the warders' houses to the street gate.

Once out on Du Cane Road, Whitey took the lead, heading straight across to where some ancient riot had trampled down the barrier which separated the road from the parallel railway line. There was no time to run right until they reached a footbridge, and to head left would bring them face to face with the armed guards who at any moment must be issuing from the end of Artillery Road.

Whether the Underground system was still functioning, he did not know. But panic took him straight over the lines, looking neither to left or right, with the others close behind. And panic kept them twisting and turning for what seemed hours through a maze of undistinguishable streets till they could run no more. Sobbing desperately for breath, they took refuge in a lane behind a row of lock-up shops, collapsing among dustbins and crates of rubbish for better concealment.

After a while, Chaucer spoke for the first time since the shooting started.

"We can't stay here," he said. "This whole bloody town's going to be after us."

"What do you suggest?" snapped the girl. "Didn't your boys have a nice escape route mapped out?"

"No doubt," said Chaucer. "But *they* had mapped it out. There'll be a car, and money, and clothes waiting somewhere, but God knows where. What a bloody cock-up!"

He smashed his right fist into his other palm in fury.

"It's your cock-up," said Whitey. "Not much subtlety, your Strikers, have they?"

"You'd be still inside if it wasn't for them," snarled Chaucer.

"Correction. If I wasn't a light sleeper. Anyway, let's try to work something out. It's over five years since I was in this town, so I've got little to contribute. What do you reckon?"

The girl interrupted. She seemed to have burnt herself completely out and spoke in accents of near-despair.

"What's the use? What can we do? As soon as it gets light, they'll spot us. Look at us, me in a kimono, you plastered like a hospital case, you in prison uniform!"

Whitey looked at the others and had to admit she was right. He was the only one wearing clothing that could pass for normal. The girl's kimono might do at a pinch, but Chaucer's grey denim with large yellow circles was impossible to modify.

He stood up.

"At least let's keep moving," he said with as much brightness as he could muster.

The girl remained slumped against a bin, but Chaucer got up.

"One thing," he said. "Why'd you come to warn me?"

Whitey shrugged.

"Everyone's entitled to one mistake."

"Thanks," said Chaucer, whether ironically or genuinely, Whitey could not tell.

"Three together's no good," said Chaucer. "We ought to split up."

"Well, off you go," said Whitey, turning away.

"I intend to," said Chaucer. Something in his voice made Whitey turn back. He caught a quick glimpse of the man's face set with effort, heard the girl begin to say something, then the warder's baton which Chaucer was swinging caught him at the base of his neck and he fell among the crates of shop rubbish.

When he awoke, the dawn had broken and thin sunlight was sliding down the dustbin lids.

He felt cold. When he shook his head, groaned at the effort and finally achieved something like normal eyesight, he realized why.

He was wearing only his underclothes. Everything else had gone. The girl had gone. Chaucer had gone.

But in a neat little pile at Whitey's feet he had left his prison suit.

Nixon Lectures : Fifth Series

Audio-Visual Material
3 (j) B.B.C. Tele-commentary: F.A. Cup, Third Round 1982

Now we're going outside the stadium to look at the scenes on the roads approaching this famous Midlands ground. As you've seen, the ground's practically full already, not more than a fraction of all these people out here can hope to get in. Those two coaches trapped in the crowd out there seem to contain visiting supporters. Thank heaven it's not the visiting team, but they've been safe in their dressing room for over an hour now. Still, I shouldn't like to be in one of those coaches, the crowd outside's looking very angry. I hope they've got the sense to keep their doors locked and sit quietly till the police can reach them and clear a way through. I hope they're quick. You can see how the crowd's rocking that front coach, it must be like a rough Channel crossing in there, this looks like a very nasty situation. You can probably hear that police siren in the background but it's a long way off and getting through this lot won't be easy. Look! Is that smoke? Oh Jesus Christ! It's on fire! Oh Jesus! I can't believe it . . . the whole length of the bus . . . wrapped in flames . . . oh Jesus Christ!

Chapter 4

The streets of London may never have been paved with gold, but at least there had been a time when it was possible to see what they *were* paved with. Now in many places rubbish from shops and houses spilled so far over the sidewalks that pedestrians were forced into the middle of the road. Sporadic collections, usually privately financed or yussed, had so far kept a passage open for motor vehicles, but fires were a constant danger and a permanent pall of smoke hung over the city.

But the dangers to health were even more basic than this. Anyone walking the streets was looking for trouble, in one sense of the phrase or another. The only law was the law of what you could get away with. At night innumerable gangs roamed around, trying their strength against each other. The man alone was everyone's victim.

Whitey had no choice, however. He had to keep moving and at five o'clock in the morning the streets were probably quieter than at any other time of day. He had done the only thing possible with Chaucer's prison suit, turning it inside out so that, while it still looked absurd from any distance up to three or four yards, at least it did not scream for attention from a couple of furlongs. But he had to find shelter before the city began to wake up and he became the object of everybody's curiosity.

At the moment it was only those who had been sent out specifically to hunt for him that he had to fear. And there might be relatively few of those.

The Governor of the Scrubs might well have restricted the search to his own personal team in the hope that he could square things without reference to the Management. The price of failure at any level could be high and to lose a prisoner of Chaucer's status as well as Singleton in one night was a pretty large failure. Not to mention the girl. Whitey realized he had no idea of her value. Why had she helped to bring the plane to England? Why had her reward been so violent? He did not even know her name. 'Hydrangea' would do, because of the eyes. Hydrangea. He ought to hate her because she was responsible that he was a fugitive in London instead of sitting on the by-lines of a nice safe war in the Sudan. Also because she seemed to have thrown in her lot with Chaucer. But the thought of her did not set the hate-glands secreting their bitter juices. Instead he hoped she was safe and well.

Such altruism gave him a self-congratulatory glow which lasted perhaps half a minute. Then the aches of hunger and battered flesh took over again.

He had been heading steadily east, navigating

by glimpses of London's tallest building, Athletic House, and occasional sightings of the burnt-out stick of the old Post Office Tower. His destination was the American Embassy, but it was a choice made for the sake of making a choice rather than from any real hope. He knew from his activities as a journalist that even if a special watch were not being kept there, the normal security team had strict orders to check all those entering or leaving. For years the Americans had regularly protested at such harassment, but the new English Diplomat had been brought up in a tougher, blunter school than the old. The word of an Englishman was once more famous throughout the world. Only the word had changed.

In any case, the Americans would be reluctant to find themselves with an 'incident' on their hands. This Embassy in Athletic Territory was their sole beachhead not only on British soil, but on European soil too. Seven years earlier after the revelation of the Hyperion series of nuclear tests in outer space, the European Parliament had broken off all relations with the U.S.A. and only in the new fragmented Britain had the Americans found a niche. Whitey knew Sam Exsmith, the Ambassador, well enough to know that he would not risk his country's standing here for the sake of a single man.

But there was nowhere else to go. He riffled through the five-year-old address book he carried in his mind and dismissed the names one after another. John Caldercote perhaps. He might be attracted by such a good though unprintable story. He had come nearest to being a close friend. But not so close that they hadn't drifted apart in the years before Whitey's arrest. It was this sense of being unable to hold anyone close which had contributed in part to his sudden marriage. He had needed someone, and the young golden haired Scottish girl he had met on that last assignment to Rangers territory had been deeply and obviously infatuated. It might have been the comparative glamour of his job. Men who could still move with some freedom round the country were rare. Or perhaps it was his reputation, already firmly established, as an outspoken attacker of the Four Club system.

Or perhaps it was just affection, which would have deepened to real love. There was no chance to find out. The Management had had enough and they were waiting for him when he returned from Glasgow with his new bride.

He had fought. It was useless, but he'd done it all the same. All the Strikers needed to do was hit him on the head once. But it is a truth proven by police forces all over the world, that if once they have guns, someone will fire. And Audrey, still too surprised to be afraid, had fallen to the ground, her golden hair spread over the airport concrete like a sunburst.

She had died in hospital they told him in his cell. He had taken no interest in anything for a while after that, existing in a trance-like state

51

even when his unknown rescuers took him from the prison hulk and laid him in the stinking bilges of the ancient loading barge which floated him downriver to freedom.

He had been letting his feet choose their own course for several minutes now as his mind drifted back over those long past events. Now he stopped, bewildered and fearing he was lost. Far from it, he realized, as the familiarity of his surroundings suddenly struck him. He had almost reached the Bayswater Road. His feet, left to their own devices, had turned off the path to the Embassy and taken him home. Two more streets only, then round a corner and there ahead was Ramsey House, the big, square undistinguished block of flats which for so many years had been home.

He heard a car approaching and stepped into a doorway. The vehicle passed the end of the street and disappeared. It was foolish to stay here, but he remained in the doorway staring at the flats, wondering what had happened to all his belongings, his papers. There had been two thirds of a novel there, never to be finished now. The man who could have finished it was long gone.

A burst of high-pitched laughter snapped him out of his reverie. Across the street the door beneath a sign saying *Klub Kocatrice* had opened and four women were pretending to be exaggeratedly dazzled by the daylight. They were extravagantly dressed in the Edwardian style which

Whitey presumed had superseded the Puritan-Maid look which had been the fashionable irony last time he was in London.

The women were crossing the road now, talking and laughing. They were heavily painted and powdered and a little drunk, so he assumed from their noise and flamboyancy. One of them spotted him and pointed. The others laughed and to his annoyance veered towards him. He stepped from the doorway and started to walk away but the woman who had pointed ran after him and seized his arm. She was a tall, bold-faced creature whose large but well-proportioned frame he might on another occasion have greatly admired. Now the strength of her grip was a cause of annoyance, not sexual excitement.

"Whither away, chuck?" she asked. "Don't you like the look of me, then?"

She ran her tongue round her lips till they glistened with saliva and with her free hand patted the gleaming red hair which was visible beneath her feather bonnet. Her companions laughed once more and began to circumambulate Whitey, inspecting him as though he were modelling some new gown hot from the designers.

"He's a bit battered," said the smallest of the four, a round-faced blonde who winked at Whitey with what seemed real friendliness.

"So he is, the poor mannikin," said the big woman. "Has some nasty reffer been beating you up?"

"Perhaps he likes it," interjected one of the others.

"Likes it? Ooh, that would be nasty. No, he doesn't look as if he likes it. In fact, I don't know who designs your clothes, my poppet, but I'd say you were running away from it."

They all peered closely at Whitey's prison clothes. The blonde fingered the material with distaste.

"Oh yes. Isn't it awful? Imagine having that next to your skin."

They went off into peals of laughter once more and Whitey, feeling the big woman's grip relax, tried to move on.

"Where are you going, my mouse?" she demanded, putting her arm over his shoulders and pressing her body close to his. "Don't leave your friends so precipitately. You need someone to look after you. We'll look after him won't we, girls?"

"Oh yes, yes," came the chorus.

"We'll find you somewhere nice to stay. Get you some nice new clothes. He'll like the clothes, won't he?"

"Oh yes!" The shrieks of laughter again, almost hysterical now. For a second Whitey had been half-tempted to regard this as a genuine offer of help. Perhaps the golden-hearted tart myth was not after all without foundation. But there was something threatening, something disturbing about these women. In some intangible way something was not quite right. The large woman pressed harder against him, almost locking his thigh between her legs. And suddenly the something not right was absolutely tangible.

He broke away with a violent effort.

"No thanks. No," he said, trying to move on. But they all pressed close now in a tight square.

"If he doesn't want protection, he must want the other thing," said the little blonde.

"I'm afraid so."

"I thought he looked bent."

Whitey looked round the compass of faces, teeth showing, eyes gleaming in anticipation of what was to come, saw the masculine run of their jaws and set of their shoulders and wondered how he could ever have seen anything else. He was sweating with fear but he tried to adopt a blustering bullying tone.

"Right, you reffing glibs," he said. "You reff off, or I'll get a couple of Supporters along to sort you out. Go on! Split!"

"Hark how he talks!" mocked the big 'woman'. "Supporters indeed. The only supporters you have will be for your hernia."

"Has he got a hernia?" asked the blonde, solicitously.

"If he hasn't, it can be arranged."

They laughed as the first blows struck home. Whitey retreated against a wall in an effort to protect his rear, but it was merely a time-saving operation. In his condition, a frontal attack from any one of them would have been almost impossible to resist. His only hope was flight. Perhaps the drink and their cumbersome clothes would slow them down enough for a short sprint to shake them off. Anything more than a short sprint was quite beyond him.

Head down, arms flailing, he launched himself from the wall, breaking through the line of assailants by the suddenness of his move. His impetus gave him a ten-yard start, but a quick glance back after thirty or forty yards showed him that the 'women' were far from averse to a chase. Skirts hilted above the knees, eyes alight with wild pleasure, they were striding after him. To a casual observer it must have been a comic sight. To Whitey it was terrifying. If they caught him, the very least he could expect was a beating which would leave him so incapacitated that recapture would be certain. As it was, his weary and bruised muscles were already shrieking their demands for instant and lengthy rest. He knew he could not outrun his pursuers. The only chance was to hide.

He flung himself right, crashing through the swing doors of Ramsey House.

Ahead of him was the lift and the stairs. On the wall between them was a list of flat numbers with the occupants' names alongside. Automatically his eyes flickered to 3.35. And stayed.

The name on the card was the same as it had been five years ago.

Singleton.

His mind was racing with crazy speculations as he headed for the stairs. Only fools and the well supported used lifts. Like any confined space they were to be avoided.

Suppose, his insane thoughts whispered as he scrambled madly up the stairs, suppose Audrey had not died; suppose that was just one more turn of the screw they had applied to him; suppose she had come out of hospital after his escape, been allowed to take possession of his old flat, kept so closely watched that she had never been able to get word out to him.

It was all quite impossible. But he had to find out. And to find out, he had to survive. Round another corner and ahead was the first floor landing. Behind him he could hear the feet of his pursuers clattering on the wooden treads.

The extra effort needed to run up the stairs had exhausted his small reserves of energy even more quickly than anticipated and he knew now that his hopes of getting far enough ahead to lose the 'women' in the maze of corridors which ran through the huge building were dim. Calling for assistance or knocking on doors was pointless. Nowadays people barred their homes like bank vaults and only opened up when convinced it was safe to do so. A strange man in a prison suit was hardly the best kind of guarantor.

He had to stop for breath and leaned up against the wall, panting hard and resting his brow on the pleasantly cool metal of the fire-extinguisher.

The following steps had also slowed down because of the ascent, but they were close now. There was little he could do. His old flat was on the next floor but one and even if he reached it, no woman used to living on her own in London was going to open the door and let him in. Force was out of the question. There just wasn't the time or the strength.

There was, however, he discovered, the time and the strength to lift the extinguisher from its bracket and to rest it on the floor at the head of the stairs. And just sufficient time and strength remained to break the plastic seal, lift the cup and depress the plunger which sent a stream of custard-yellow foam into the face of the blonde as 'she' rounded the corner. It unseated the hat and wig revealing a basin-cropped mousy stubble before the foam replaced the errant blonde wig with a fell of yellow bubbles.

Perhaps this witless fate which has got me into this mess is now arranging for me to slide out of it, thought Whitey and instantly put his thesis to the test by crashing his elbow through the glass panel next to the fire-extinguisher bracket and pressing the alarm button.

As he laboriously dragged himself up the stairs to the third floor, he thought of Audrey (he was sure now it would be Audrey) roused from her early morning half-sleep by the siren's shriek, getting out of bed, looking through the window in an effort to spot smoke, slipping on a dressing gown, pausing before the mirror to make sure that she was presentable to the outside world, then making her way to the main door of the flat to begin the complicated business of releasing the multiplicity of bolts and locks which kept her safe and cosy through the night. If fate had done a face-about, she would be the first in her corridor to open the door and peer out and she would do this just as he arrived.

It went as pre-ordained. He felt no surprise at seeing the handle turn as he limped towards the door; he accelerated, confident that his arrival was going to be perfectly timed; and his shoulder hit the door just as the night-gowned woman within became aware of his approach and tried to slam it shut.

The force of his entry bowled her over and sent her crashing across the polished floor of the entrance hall.

Whitey nearly followed suit, but managed to retain his balance and crash the door shut behind him just as other doors up and down the corridor began to open and disgorge their fire-terrified inmates into unprecedented confrontations with each other.

Whitey leaned against the door, sliding home bolts and saying a little prayer of thanks to his new friend, Fate. Then he turned to face his wife.

The woman cowered on the floor, hardly able to move, clearly fearing the worst. Or perhaps not that. When a desperate-looking man forced his way into a woman's flat in the early hours of the morning, even the best was fearful enough.

But the terror on her face was well matched by the disappointment on Whitey's.

He had never seen this woman before in his life.

Nixon Lectures: Fifth Series

Documentary Material

3 (b) Extract from 'Civil Strife and Football:' The Report of a Committee of Enquiry appointed by the Secretary of State for Home Affairs: 1983

It is with considerable regret that the Commission concludes that the only solution to the grave problem before us is a suspension *sine die* of the playing of Association Football at all levels. It is our hope that the social climate may so change that a review of this ban may be possible within a few years.

It is also recommended that the stadia and their facilities be leased to the many official Supporters Clubs in the hope that they will become social centres and strong influences for stability.

Chapter 5

"It's all right," said Whitey. "I'm not going to hurt you."

He nodded reassuringly at the woman and pressed his ear to the door in a vain attempt to learn what was happening outside. Only the howl of the fire-alarm pierced the four inches of solid plas-teak which modern living required as standard thickness for an outer door.

It didn't matter. The glibs would hardly hang around to be investigated by the building's security team. And there was no reason for anyone to check this particular flat, not even the Scrubs Strikers. Not now that it appeared it wasn't his wife's. *Felix culpa,* he told himself smugly, turning back to the woman.

She had gone.

Through the open lounge door he saw her, telephone in hand, staring at him with a desperate impatience in her face which told him she had not yet been connected.

This is what came of sounding reasonable, he told himself as he moved towards her. His little bit of reassurance had merely given her strength to head for the 'phone.

His hand smashed down on the rest. He put his face close to hers.

"Another trick like that and I'll tear you in half," he said.

That worked nicely. She slid weakly to the floor, dropping the receiver. He picked it up and replaced it on the stand.

"Just stay there," he said. "Answer when you're spoken to. Do what I tell you to. Otherwise just sit. Right? One wrong move and you're relegated."

It was the authentic note. This was a scene every woman living alone must have rehearsed. All that was necessary was to remember the right lines.

He made a quick tour of the flat. One thing became clear. He had made no mistake. This had been his flat. The decor had been altered but there were still things he could remember. The M-shaped crack in the ceiling plaster which always opened up no matter how often you filled it. The creaking board one pace through the kitchen door. The Athletic red bathroom suite, complete with First Team portrait tiles, the choice of a previous occupant. He looked at the row of shiny faces and smiled, recalling how expert he had become at toothpaste graffiti.

"I'm a good Supporter."

It was the woman's voice, pleading and fearful. She had been following his progress round the flat and seeing him pause so long at the red bathroom door, obviously hoped he would be impressed.

"I told you to keep tight," Whitey snapped.

"Till I ask questions, which is now. How long have you lived here?"

"I don't know. Four, five years."

"Four, five years," repeated Whitey. "Interesting. Who had it before you?"

"I don't know," she said.

"Come on, girlie! Just throw your mind back. Who had it before you?"

"I don't know. It was empty when I moved in. I never saw the other people!"

She was close to hysteria in her effort to convince him. Whitey felt sick at the thought of being able to frighten someone into this state, yet it was not only sickness he felt. He turned back to the bathroom unwilling to face the girl, and looked at himself reflected in the bright red tiles like a spirit in Hades.

"That name list in the entrance-hall," he said. "It says someone called Singleton lives here."

"Does it? I never bothered to put my name up when I came. My friends know where I live."

Perhaps I'm less famous than I think, thought Whitey. But surely someone in the block would have let her know she was occupying the one-time residence of the great criminal, Whitey Singleton?

He dismissed the speculation as idle. The thing now was to rest up for a while. He was very hungry and very tired. It was quite hard to focus his eyes on the girl who sat before him, head bowed, like a Pre-Raphaelite model posing for Despair.

63

"Come here," he commanded.

Slowly she rose. She was, he reckoned, in her late twenties, not pretty, but not plain either. Terror is quite becoming, he decided, if you have the bone structure to support it.

"What's your name?"

"Nancy Mays," she said with difficulty as though she found it hard to remember.

"Right, Nancy. I'm going to ask you a few questions. Be sure you answer them truthfully for if I discover you've been lying about anything at all, I shall kill you."

Even a mere quarter of a century earlier, the majority of Englishmen would have been unable to take such a threat completely seriously. At least not without guns being pointed, knives waved, the whole context of violence in evidence. But now incredulity was no longer the enemy of the threatener. Now anyone would believe anything of anyone.

"You live here by yourself, Nancy?"

"Yes."

That fitted with what he had seen in his quick look round.

"Do you have a job, Nancy?"

"Yes."

"Clever girl. What time do you start work?"

"Ten."

He glanced at the old wooden wall-clock above the bathroom door. It was still only 5-30 A.M., he was surprised to note. Days seemed to have passed since he awoke and discovered Chaucer

64

and the girl had gone.

"Will you be missed if you don't turn up?"

She hesitated.

"I mean, will any effort be made to contact you. Come on. You must know!"

"They might . . . I mean, someone could ring, just to see . . ."

"Yes."

That made sense. And if no one answered, would they come round to check for themselves? Hardly. But it was still a risk.

He found himself yawning and pressed on.

"Is there any reason why anybody should call here this morning. Delivery men? Cleaner? Anyone like that."

"No."

"You're certain."

"Certain!"

She sounded almost indignant.

"All right," he said. "Just hope no one rings that bell. Now listen. I'm going to be around here for a while. You go into the bathroom and shut the door behind you. No noise, mind. And don't try to come out till I tell you. Any noise or any attempt to get out and that'll be it. Understand?"

She nodded.

"In you go."

She obeyed. He removed the key from inside the door which he then closed and locked. Next he took a chair and hung it over the door handle, jamming its legs up against the wall. It was the best he could do, he decided. The bathroom itself had no window and even if she plucked up enough courage to rap on the one wall which was connected to a neighbouring flat, it was doubtful whether anyone would care to take notice. Anyway, it was a risk he'd have to take.

Of course, he found himself thinking, I really could kill her.

With a sigh, he shook his head and went into the kitchen. Food first. There was a plentiful supply of tins and he ate his way through four of them almost indiscriminately. Then he returned to the lounge, checked the bathroom door, lay down on the comfortable old-fashioned settee, and went to sleep.

The Dream came almost instantly. It had taken two and a half years of twice-weekly analysis to erase it from his subconscious. The consultant had modestly claimed complete success and charged the appropriate fee, but Whitey had never really doubted that the snake was merely scotched. Now as the old familiar images returned from their long exile, some still wakeful part of his mind greeted them if not with pleasure, at least with that fascinated revulsion which draws the sensitive child back again and again to the storybook which he knows will give him nightmares. It was not until the coach in front exploded in flames and the screams of those trapped inside were momentarily audible above the roar of the mob that this small standpoint of objectivisation crumbled and he was wholly fourteen once more and feeling a terror which acted as the yardstick for all other terrors he had felt since that day.

He awoke with the usual violent surge like a dolphin breaking clear of the water. It was the image that usually came to his mind and he found it of little comfort to think that to him his waking life might be as relatively brief as those few moments free of the water were to the leaping sea-mammal.

Despite his feeling that the Dream had occupied every second of the time since he lay down, two hours had passed. He was hungry again and returned to the kitchen, eating rather more selectively this time. A stiff drink of some kind would have gone down well also, but the liquor cupboard was either empty, well-concealed or non-existent, and he settled for a pot of coffee instead. A twinge of conscience, or perhaps just a need to establish that his conscience was still capable of twinging, made him pour a cup for the girl. He removed the chair from the doorknob and rapped on the woodwork, feeling rather ridiculous.

"Like some coffee?" he called. There was no reply, which did not surprise him, and he unlocked the door.

The jet of water that hit him from the shower attachment in the girl's hands was not hot enough to blister but it burnt his beaten face like acid and sent him staggering backwards over a chair.

She leapt over him and made for the hall. By the time he rose and followed, she was more than halfway through the complicated business of unlocking the door. He would still have had plenty of time to stop her if he had acted straightaway but at the sight of him she started screaming, her hands still busy at the door. Absurdly, he halted and started trying to reason with her. She turned the handle, the door began to open, now he jumped forward to throw his weight against it. But a greater weight at the other side thrust against him and he fell back.

Standing in the door, crouched aggressively, was a man. In his hand was an automatic pointed straight at Whitey's head.

"Don't move," he said. "Not an inch. Audrey, are you OK?"

"Yes," said the girl, sobbing with relief. Then the strength seemed to leave her legs and she slid down the wall in a dead faint.

"John Caldercote," said Whitey suddenly.

The man stiffened, then peered more closely at his bruised face.

"Whitey?" he said uncertainly. "Whitey Singleton?"

"That's it," said Whitey, pushing himself upright. "What did you call her?"

He pointed at the recumbent girl.

"What the hell's going on here?" demanded Caldercote. "What are you doing here anyway? And don't say you've forgotten your wife!"

Nixon Lectures: Fifth Series

Documentary Material

2 (k) Extract from minutes of British Trade Union Congress. 1984. Mr. Fred Burdern (head of the Federation of Supporters Clubs) proposing motion of no confidence in the Government.

Brothers, I put it to you plainly. This is more than just a motion of no-confidence we are debating. We've already put on record our determination not to recognize this law. But it seems to me to follow that if you don't recognize the law, you don't recognize the law-givers.

Brothers, if we pass this motion, it means more than we just want the buggers out. It means that if the buggers *don't* get out, then as far as we're concerned, this country's without a government and we'll bloody well have to govern ourselves! (N.B. Motion passed nem. con.)

Chapter 6

John Caldercote had put on weight and the light brown worsted suit that he loaned to Whitey hung round him like a collapsed soufflé.

His extra weight had not prevented him from moving with an urgency just short of panic when he realized the implications of what he'd found at Ramsey House.

"Not your wife!" he'd kept on repeating. "Reff me! Not your wife!"

The girl had recovered from her faint, realized her 'rescuer' had been won over to the opposition, and withdrew into a terrified silence.

"She must be a plant. All these years. Oh Christ, what a lot that explains!"

Caldercote had tied her up so brutally that Whitey had protested.

"She's lucky," retorted the angry man. "The Jays will be furious I didn't kill her. Christ, and to think I went rushing round like the bearer of love-tidings to tell her you were back in town."

"You knew?"

"Infiltration works both ways."

There had been no question in Caldercote's mind but that he had to get out. They had driven furiously to his flat where he had parked the car for a few minutes while he went in to collect a few important papers and also some clothes for Whitey. Then a quick 'phone call. A risk, he admitted, but what the hell? It was possible they were being trailed already, and he needed instructions.

"From who?" asked Whitey, bewildered.

"You don't know. Things have come a long way since we got you out, Whitey. In a way, that was almost the start."

"You were in on that?"

"Of course. It was after that that the Jays began to appear. I've stayed on the surface, fooling everybody so I reckoned. But when Audrey or whatever her name is turned up, well, I sniffed around for a few months, then casually made contact."

"But for God's sake, you'd never seen her before."

"Exactly. Nobody had. We read that his young wife had been brutally sacrificed by the traitor Singleton in his attempts to escape. We checked on the hospital. She was there. After a while, she became visitable and we sent someone in to take a look. It was the girl in the flat, no doubt. And she's been patched up from gunshot wounds. I've seen the scars."

"Oh yes," said Whitey neutrally.

"Yes. I'm sorry. But five years is a long time, Whitey, and what's it matter now anyway? When we were convinced she was with us, we tried to get her out to join you. But things went wrong. We lost half a dozen men. She must have set it

71

up herself, the bitch! After that she said she didn't want out, didn't want anyone else killed on her behalf! And she made a special thing of asking that you shouldn't be told about her. Your new life, your protests on the outside, these were too important to jeopardize. Christ, she had me crying nearly!"

"And Audrey?"

"Died in hospital, I suppose. And some bright reffer got the notion of playing a substitute."

They relapsed into silence. The car they were in was weaving a complicated web around North London. Its licence plate did not permit it to move outside certain clearly defined metropolitan limits, but at least they could make sure they were not being followed within that area. The towers of Wembley Stadium were visible from time to time and once they found themselves moving steadily down Olympic Way towards the huge structure itself. The dull red Athletic banners fluttered gently from every flagpole and on the steps leading up to the stadium the usual groups of strikers and supporters were standing. Whitey held his breath till the car turned away and left them behind.

"Tell me," said Whitey. "How long have you been running these, what do you call them, Jays?"

Caldercote laughed.

"You flatter me. I don't run them. They run me. I was approached very discreetly, about four years ago. I'd thought I was a real counter-revolutionary after your escape. But I was beginning to realize there wasn't any counter revolution. Just a few individuals making a lot of noise."

"And now?"

"We still make a lot of noise, but not with our mouths. Our people aren't the only ones who've been taken out."

"On Christ." Whitey stared glumly out of the side window. They were passing down a street of mean terraced houses. No one was in sight. Only an occasional dog or rat moved behind the piles of uncollected rubbish.

"I thought that violence and terror were what you were fighting against," he observed neutrally.

"What else? But it takes a diamond to cut a diamond. And the pen is only mightier than the sword till someone chops your nib off."

"Is that so? Well, at least I'm glad to see you haven't forgotten how to hide the truth in metaphor."

John stabbed down angrily on the accelerator and the car surged forward through an amber light.

"You can be smug, Whitey. You've been out of it for five years, playing at real journalism. It works if the system lets it work, that's true. I've read some of your pieces that have been smuggled in. They've been good, very good. Only, never forget that if anybody's caught reading them over here, they'll be yussed away so fast they won't have time to crap themselves through terror!"

"Steady," said Whitey. "Do they still have speed limits?"

The car slowed down to a respectable pace once more.

"Where are we going?"

"Somewhere safe."

"Hold it," said Whitey. "You're certain you've got somewhere safe to take me? It wouldn't be anywhere Miss Nancy Mays knew about, would it?"

"I doubt it," said John. "It's somewhere even I don't know about."

They drove swiftly west now, changing cars three times as they reached licensing limits. Restriction had already begun to exist five years earlier, but they had developed considerably since Whitey's departure. At each limit, they got out, moved quickly into the next car and drove on. The abandoned car was driven away behind them, but only once did Whitey catch a glimpse of the exchange driver, a nondescript youth wound round with an Athletic scarf and looking like a thousand other supporters.

"We work on two levels," explained John. "There are those of us who have a position in the overground. And there's the true underground, those who either through choice or necessity work at it full time. The two levels are linked, of course, but we only know how to use the links. An undergrounder can never betray the identity of an overgrounder, nor an overgrounder

74

betray the location of an underground hide-out."

"So Nancy couldn't know where we're going?"

"Right. But she did know about me, which is why I'm going with you."

"Why the panic?"

"When they find her, they're not going to muck about. Before, they were happy to pick us off one by one, trying not to excite too much suspicion. Now there'll be one great sweep. I've sent the word out, but it won't reach everybody in time."

A thoughtful silence followed.

"Because of me," said Whitey finally.

"Don't flatter yourself," said John. "Nearly there."

There turned out to be Oxford. It seemed a rather too obvious place for a centre of subversion, thought Whitey uneasily. If he were in charge of the anti-guerrilla team, Oxford would be one of the first spots to be cleaned out. It was at the far edge of Athletic territory, close to the border of the Midlands area run by Wanderers. This proximity in itself was no great advantage to the Underground; if there was any single thing the Four Clubs who ruled most of England were agreed on, it was a common policy against subversives. Wanderers Supporters might be reluctant to hand Whitey back to the jurisdiction of Athletic, but only because they would like the pleasure of dealing with him themselves.

For all that, Oxford and places like it did have something of the feel of frontier towns, a restlessness and wildness, which could cover a man's passage very quickly. And in addition the presence of the University was still felt, though like all other institutions of higher education, it had been formally dissolved eight years earlier. The colleges remained as Supporters' Clubs, but they still attracted mainly the young; and curiously the traditional medieval town and gown tensions, moribund for many centuries, had started back to life as the University died. The colleges regarded themselves as a kind of Athletic Red Guard. Their centre was All Souls (hence the local sobriquet of 'assoles', for the young Supporters); and rampaging bands of these assoles roamed the streets, ready to yuss anybody whose loyalty to the Club did not appear as absolute as their own.

Thus in Oxford and places like it, the kind of social stasis which existed in most large centres of population was never achieved. And this in itself made it a place to look at with considerable suspicion, from everybody's point of view, thought Whitey uneasily.

They drove uninterrupted across Magdalen Bridge and parked in the High opposite Queen's. 'Parked' was perhaps too precise a word. John just stopped the car, got out and started walking briskly towards Carfax. Whitey had to trot to catch up with him.

"What happens now?" he panted.

"We'll be contacted," said John cheerily.

They were, almost immediately. As they passed All Souls, a small group of Supporters, sitting on the pavement, rose, crossed the road and fell into step alongside them.

"Where's your colours, squire?" enquired one of them, thrusting his sallow, unshaven face very close to Whitey's. John thrust him away with an open-handed push.

"In the wash," he said looking down at his hand in disgust. "You ought to try it some time."

"A joker!" said the stubbly Supporter in mock-awe. "A laugh-a-minute man, I say I say, entertainer of thousands. I've picked myself a reffing clown!"

They were passing the end of the Turl. Whitey was beginning to feel very unhappy. To get involved with these boys could mean more than just a physical yussing. He had heard tales of people subjected to a twenty-four hour examination by a so-called disciplinary committee. The pressures so exerted could bring even a genuine Supporter to an admission of disloyalty. Whitey felt himself in no fit state either mentally or physically to withstand such an ordeal. But John showed no inclination to be conciliatory.

"Keep it up son," he mocked. "You might make the reserves some day if you grow up and one or two other miracles happen. Meanwhile, why don't you run along like a nice little assole?"

Whitey felt himself seized from behind, saw John grabbed likewise, screamed as his arms were forced up towards his shoulder blades and made no effort to resist as he was bundled across the road, up the Turl and through a door into Jesus

College. Once inside there was no pause in his precipitous progress. He was rushed across a quadrangle, through another door, up a narrow flight of stairs on which he stumbled several times only to be wrenched upright with muscle-tearing force, and finally through yet another door which this time led into a room. His arms were released and the pain of their reverting to their normal position was almost as bad as the pain which preceded it. He sank on his knees and rocked gently to and fro, some ridiculous pride making him bite back the groans which were trying to force a way out.

"Caldercote and Singleton," said a voice. Whitey glanced up. It was the stubbly supporter. He was speaking to a man sitting at his ease in an old wing-chair before a large open fireplace in which a pot of geraniums burnt brighter than coal. He was about twenty years old, wearing a red and white striped blazer, matching shirt, and a huge Athletic rosette. His pale round face bore a sombre disapproving expression as he regarded the two newcomers, but his voice was studiedly neutral as he repeated, "Caldercote and Singleton."

"I'm Caldercote," said John who seemed to have suffered rather less in the transfer from the street.

"I know," said the young man. "I'm King."

Whether this was a title or a name, Whitey could not make out. He did not care much either.

"You mean, this is it?" he demanded of Caldercote, half relieved, half angry. He rose and turned on the stubbly youth. "You overdid the realism a bit, didn't you?"

"Singleton," said King. "You're not much like your picture." He had a copy of *Nuspic* in his hand.

"People change," grunted Whitey.

"So they say. Caldercote, why did you ask for transfer?"

Rapidly John explained the situation. King listened without interrupting.

At the end he said, "So you're finished overground. Let's hope you're not too old to learn new tricks."

"Not so new!" said John with a slightly over-hearty laugh. "Why, I was active . . ."

"Fine, fine. Georgie, take him down to the buttery and find what he can do. We'll talk later."

The stubbly youth led John to the door in a manner which brooked no refusal. There was a lengthy silence after they had gone. Whitey made his way to an armchair and sat down, uninvited. Besides King, there were two others in the room, of much the same age. They stood, very still, on either side of the lace-curtained window.

Whitey made a conscious effort to control the irrational pique he had felt at his rough handling. It was absurd. He had been hurt much more than this in the past twenty-four hours, and these men were responsible for his present safety. So why should he feel so antagonistic?

He was able to answer himself almost immediately. Because they were young. Because he resented having to feel indebted to these callow youths who had been mere babes in arms when he crouched by his father's side, terrified by the menacing faces pressed against the coach window, and saw the flames leap up from the road ahead.

"I'm grateful to you for arranging this," he heard himself say, pleasantly if rather formally, through the edges of the waking nightmare.

"Spare us the thanks," said King. "It's a way out from overground. Caldercote needed it. You just happened to be along."

Whitey should have felt happy to be thus absolved from feeling gratitude. He didn't.

"What happens now?" he asked.

"Who knows?" answered King.

"That's a good question," said Whitey. "Why not take me to someone who does know?"

He stood up, suddenly impatient to be away from this round-faced youth in the fancy dress.

"So you're Singleton," said King.

"Yes, I'm Singleton and I'd like to talk with someone who matters." He let his anger show now.

"You know where you are, Singleton?"

"Yes," he said, startled by the inconsequentiality of the question.

"Where?"

"Jesus College, Oxford. Of course! The Jays! You might as well advertise!"

"And you've met me."

"So?"

80

King's voice was low, controlled.

"I'd like to chuck you back, Singleton. Drop you where we found you. Only now you know about Jesus. It's not a joke, so don't put on your non-smiling look. All the good Jesus jokes were made years ago. I'm serious. You know what Jesus is? It's the centre of our movement. Unless age has calcined your grey matter even more than indicated by the wishy-washy crap you write, you've been able to work something like that out for yourself. And I place no great reliance in your capacity for silence. So we must do something else with you."

Whitey felt a white heat of rage explode in his head. The kind of angry, intolerant, arrogant words he had often vowed never to speak came bubbling out of him like lava from a crater.

"Do you know who I am? What I've done? Do you know *anything*, you little runt? I'm Singleton. I was fighting the Management before you had your first erection — if you've managed one yet. I was in the hulks while you were still spending your pocket-money on comics. I've spent all my working life telling the world the truth about this country, and there's been no occasion to mention *you*, or the likes of you. Now I want to talk to someone who really matters, *Mister* King, some-one I've heard of, not the office boy."

He cooled down as suddenly as he had erupted. Enough was enough. He felt partly ashamed, but partly glad. An organization which could exercise control over someone he respected as much as John Caldercote must have a high-powered hierarchy. Underlings like King needed to be repressed from time to time.

The youth spoke again. He did not sound repressed.

"Rest assured I've heard of you," he said. "You belong in the history books. I wish you'd stayed there. Your yesterday's hero, Singleton. No good to anyone. Those who didn't get arrested and who stayed on here, like Caldercote, they've served a purpose. But not you. All you did was set up a nice situation for the Management to exploit. That's it."

"That wasn't my responsibility," said Whitey, resentfully finding himself on the defensive. "And if I'd stayed, I'd have been dead by now. For five years, I've been the best voice you've had in the outside world . . ."

"How have you spoken for us?" demanded King scornfully. "What have you got to do with us? You've just said you never gave people like us a single mention. The Jays did not exist when you were last here. We are nothing of your creation, Singleton."

"We want the same things," averred Whitey. "We have a common aim."

"Which is?"

"To overthrow the Management! To break the stranglehold the Four Clubs have on this country."

"A broad aim," said King. "More important is, what is going to take its place? Do we have that in common too? I doubt it if I interpret this pap right!"

He slapped his copy of *Nuspic* contemptuously.

"And what of methods, Singleton? Does writing this stuff achieve anything?"

"We each use the method we're most adept at," answered Whitey tightly.

"Giving each other moral support the whiles?" mocked King. "Last night we used the method we're most adept at. We hit the house of an Athletic assistant trainer. We took the reffer alive which was what we wanted, but his wife and two daughters got shot up in the process. Do you raise your glass to that, brother-in-the-cause?"

"No. No, I don't," said Whitey wearily. "I raise my glass to the faint glimmer of hope that such things still seem to bother you a bit, son. That's all."

"What a perceptive little liberal it is," said King. "Take him away and let me get on with the day's real business. We'll talk again later when I feel like another laugh."

He made a small, weary, but imperious gesture with his right hand and for a second looked like the young state-burdened monarch his name suggested. Then the two henchmen moved forward and without touching Whitey nevertheless carried him from the room.

It would have been soothing to his self-esteem had his mind now been full of the philosophical implications of this brief conversation, but instead all he could focus on was his immediate future. The days when he would have been an honoured guest of the underground had clearly long since past. But just how precarious his position really was had not yet become clear. The two youths by his side said nothing and a mixture of apprehension and pride made him keep silent also. His main comfort was that King had said they would talk again later. *When I feel like a laugh,* he had added. Small comfort!

His two custodians halted beside a door and Whitey followed suit. The youths looked a little uncertain.

"In here?" asked one of them.

"Why not? He won't want him wandering round, will he? Kill two birds."

Just a proverb, Whitey assured himself as they knocked on the door which was cautiously opened by another young man with a submachine-gun.

No one gets sentenced with a proverb, he joked inwardly as they ushered him inside where yet another gunman stood, looking very alert and ready to act. The room was a small sitting room, not unlike the one in which he had met King. Opening off it was a bedroom whose door was wedged open revealing a man sitting slumped in an armchair and another figure lying motionless on a single bed.

"Singleton," said Georgie.

"He's to go in here? You sure? I'd better check."

He picked up the 'phone. Through the open

door Whitey saw the short thickset man in the chair look up. His face was a mass of contusions. Then the man on the bed swung his long legs wearily to the floor and rubbed his eyes.

"Yes," said the guard on the 'phone. "Yes, he has. OK." He turned to the others.

"He says to put him in."

A push in the back propelled Whitey unwillingly through the door. Protective custody was one thing, but he had little desire for his status here to be on a level with that of the men he saw before him.

"Life is rich with small surprises, Mr. Singleton," said Sheldrake. "Preds."

Nixon Lectures : Fifth Series

Audio-Visual Material

4 (L) Tape of interchange between Metropolitan Police Control and a patrol car on duty along the route of the anti-government protest march, January 1985.

Voice A Bravo 8 to Control.

Voice B Pass your message Bravo 8.

Voice A We are parked at the corner of Church Lane and Lordship Lane. We can see the demo. march coming down Lordship Lane. There's a lot of them. Request instructions.

Voice B Wait . . Bravo 8. Instructions are unchanged. Observe and control.

Voice A You must be joking! Look, there's thousands of 'em. It's more like a football crowd than a protest march. They're trotting in formation. Christ, it's frightening! Request assistance.

Voice B Observe proper procedure, Bravo 8. Wait.

Voice C Bravo 8. This is Superintendent Bass. What's the trouble? You've got your instructions?

Voice A Yes, sir. We were requesting assistance, sir.

Voice C Where the hell do you expect assistance from? These marches are going on all over London, you know that. Do your job and don't waste my time! Understand?

PAUSE

Voice C Bravo 8, I asked you, do you understand?

Voice A Oh, we understand all right, Bass. Listen, you can't see this lot, but we can. And I'll tell you this, you want this lot controlled, you'd better get yourself down here and reffing well control them yourself. Smatch!

End of tape.

Chapter 7

"May I introduce Fred Burdern," said Sheldrake. "He's not feeling very well. These wankers have been working him over for hours."

The stocky man glowered at Whitey but said nothing.

"He doesn't like you, Singleton," said Sheldrake cheerily.

"I seem fated to be locked up with Management men who don't like me," observed Whitey.

Sheldrake laughed cynically.

"You're such an obvious plant, Singleton! If they stuck you try the garden, you'd grow. How the hell did you get here? I left you in the Scrubs."

"Coincidence," said Whitey. "That's where I left you too."

"All right," said Sheldrake. "Swops. I was misguided enough to call on Fred here. He's the Club Trainer, as if you didn't know. We got taken at his house. My fault really. I showed my pass, Fred's Striker opened the gate, and these reffers were in like a bloody flash. That's all I know."

He rubbed the back of his head gingerly.

"There was a lot of gunfire. Then they came back with Fred and tossed us both into the back of a van. Nice people you're associating with, pal. They murdered the Striker at the gate and God knows who else got hurt."

King's words came back to Whitey. He must have been talking about Burdern's wife and daughters. Poor bastard, he thought looking at the man with new sympathy.

"Why did they want you?" he asked. "Hostages?"

"Oh no. Fred's our Trainer. There's a big anti-Jay operation being launched by the Strikers and Fred's the man who knows the details. That's what they want."

"They haven't bothered you much."

"Fortunately I *don't* know the details and they seem to know enough about us to know I don't know. The wankers must have someone on the inside. No, I was just a lucky bonus. Me they will use as a hostage. I hope."

He laughed, a little nervously.

"Though from your performance they hardly need to trade hostages for prisoners, do they? That old sod in the Scrubs must have crapped himself when he found you'd gone. You cost his predecessor his job and that was just by escaping from the hulks. They'll really relegate this one for letting you get out of the main gaol!"

This confirmed Whitey's own feeling that the manhunt had not been as massive and thorough an operation as the escape of Chaucer, Hydrangea and himself had merited. To alert the First Team would mean alerting the Management and the Governor had good reason for not doing that.

Memory of Hydrangea brought back to him what now seemed the incredibly distant events of the previous day.

"Did you know I was on that plane, Sheldrake?" he asked. "What was the hi-jacking all about?"

Sheldrake laughed again. He seemed incredibly relaxed for a man in his position.

"Good try, Mr. Singleton. I'm not sure why you're in here with me, but I've got to assume you're trying to catch me offside, haven't I? I mean, basically you and this lot are on the same team, aren't you? So, I don't mind a chat, but nothing confidential, you understand. Just a general picture."

"All right," said Whitey. "We'll swop general pictures. It wasn't this lot who got me out. Someone came for Chaucer. The girl and I just followed."

"All three of you broke?" Sheldrake whistled. "They'll put the old sod beyond re-election!"

"We separated," said Whitey, feeling the lump on the back of his head throb. "Eventually I was picked up by the Jays and brought here. They don't quite know what to do with me."

"That was a *very* general picture!" said Sheldrake. "All it deserves in return is the assurance that you were just a lucky bonus from the hi-jack. It wasn't all laid on for your sole benefit."

"I thought not. But why then? Why was the girl put away? What happened to the others?"

"Ref knows," said Sheldrake calmly. "I'm just an Assistant Manager."

He was lying. He knew a great deal more, Whitey was sure.

"What are you in this for, Sheldrake?" he asked curiously.

"What's a nice fellow like me doing in a joint like this, you mean?"

"Something like that. You're an intelligent man. You can see as clearly as I can that this country's reached its lowest depth since the Norman conquest. The only law is what you can get away with. The only rule of behaviour is trust no-one. The country's carved up into four unnatural territories, many of whose occupants are ready to kill each other for wearing the wrong-coloured scarf. The individual has no rights, no protection, except what he makes for himself. We're the disgrace of Europe. The only country in the civilized world which permits the basest passions, the most depraved elements, the lowest common denominators to control its destiny!"

"You should take a closer look at the rest of civilization," said Sheldrake cynically. "Listen to me, Singleton. You've been indulging in a monologue for five years without interruption and you've got used to being applauded every time you break wind. You've set yourself up as the only true chronicler of our hard times. Articles, seminars, lectures, oh yes, we hear about them, read them, look at transcripts. Then forget them.

"We're too busy surviving here. That's what

it's all about. Now you come along with your reffing condescension, appealing to my intelligence — yes, that's what it is, condescension! You mean that I seem quite bright for a management moron. Shall I tell you something? I'm fifteen years older than you. I remember the old education system well. This place we're in now, I was up at this very college, would you believe that? A historian, no less. And the one lesson that remains from my studies is that there are no cures for mankind's ailments. It's like the common cold. My granny used to say the best thing to do was take nowt, but sweat it out. If you suppressed the symptoms today, they'd just break out again next week.

"Well, even in those days, the papers and magazines and tele programmes were full of bleating sheep like you, all trying to sound like collies and telling us what was wrong with society. Why, some of you even dignified your bletherings with pseudo-scientific names and invented a new Babylonish dialect in case people should too easily detect the emptiness of your prattle!"

"You're strangely bitter," interjected Whitey. "I use no jargon. I make a simple claim for rational behaviour and the rule of law."

"And when you've said that you believe you've said something meaningful! Words and phrases like that are the faeces of the intellect. Noisome waste that needs to be flushed away. Society wisely ignores its self-elected wise men. Charlatans, wizards, witch-doctors, that's all you are,

chanting nonsense at a summer's sky and claiming huge kudos if it happens to rain."

"And what do people like yourself do, assistant
managers and historians manqués?"

"We ride the storm but don't claim to control
it. We sweat it out. We encourage the symptoms
to burn out the disease. But that's not all. I'm
falling into your trick of letting language control
meaning. It's not all disease. There's something
of robust good health here too. There's a meaning to life, a core of belief, something to treasure
and worship and fight for, such as this country
hasn't had for too reffing long!"

Whitey laughed now, as convincingly as he
could, but his amusement was drowned by a
droning noise from Burdern. For a second he
thought the man was in pain. Then he realized
he was singing, and suddenly Sheldrake joined
in and the words became clear. *Onward goes Athletic! The greatest and the best!*

It was the official Athletic anthem.

The noise brought the two guards to the door
with guns upraised. The men ignored them but
went on to the end of the verse. When they
finished Sheldrake looked from Whitey to the
guards.

"You're nothing, Singleton. You know that?
You weren't picked up as a danger but as an
occasional irritant. You're peripheral. I've more
time for this lot than you. They're part of it,
necessary. You're nothing!"

Calmly he sat down on the bed once more and

took a sip of his cold coffee. Whitey who during the song had felt a whole volcano of angry abuse and argument welling up inside himself suddenly went off the boil. It no longer seemed worth it. Abstract debate in such potentially dangerous circumstances was a mere time-waster. A logical prognosis of his situation would be a much more worthwhile achievement.

In a way, he thought gloomily, Sheldrake was much better off. A straightforward exchange for money or prisoners, and he'd go home. If the Manager thought he was worth it, that was. And if the Jays kept their bargains.

Burdern spoke again, his puffed lips distorting the words.

"What?" said Sheldrake. "Oh, the time. Christ knows. Lunch time, I suppose. What's the matter, Fred?"

Burdern glared at Whitey, then tried to whisper something in Sheldrake's ear, but the Assistant Manager couldn't make it out. He put his arm round Burdern's shoulders and led him to the furthermost corner where a bout of vigorous whispering took place. At the end of it, Sheldrake nodded his head thoughtfully.

"Very clever, Fred. Yes, that would be wise, very wise."

"What?" asked Whitey.

"Fred thinks we're talking to you too much, that's all," said Sheldrake. "You're going to Coventry."

He smiled amiably, but Whitey felt uneasy.

94

There was something here he didn't like. He went to the door and addressed the immediately alert guard.

"I want to see King."

"Your wish is my command," said King appearing at the outer door. "Burdern, you're the cunning one, aren't you? You know what he's just said, Singleton? That he's got a homing device stitched into his gut. We checked, of course, but this wanker's clever. He didn't activate it till we'd finished the first round of questioning. Fortunately we've got listening devices just as sensitive, pick up whispers even. He was telling Sheldrake here to be ready to rush the guard at the first sound of attack. Good advice. He knows that the first thing we do when attacked is kill our prisoners."

Georgie came into the room at the trot.

"There's a big concentration of Strikers building up in Cowley," he gasped.

"How big?"

"Two fifty. Three hundred."

"Flattering," said King. "They must have a fix. And when they move, they move quickly. We've got to give it to them, they're well trained."

Burdern reacted to the gibe by flinging himself forward, his hands stretched out towards King, but he contrived to get tangled up with Sheldrake and the two men fell to the floor.

King, unmoved by the attempted assault, turned away, saying to the guards, "Say good-bye to these two for me."

"What about him?" asked one of the guards, nodding at Whitey. King stared at him for a long silent four or five seconds. Whitey suddenly felt a strong urge to drop to his knees and start pleading for his life. Instead he remained upright and stared back at King with as much indifference as he could muster. It was the right reaction. King said, "Let him come with me."

Whitey caught up with him in the corridor outside.

"What will happen to those two?" he demanded boldly, trying to compensate for his own recognized fear of the previous minute.

Behind them from the room they had just left came a short clatter of gunfire. Whitey stopped and looked back, but King continued with uninterrupted pace.

"Why?" called Whitey after him. "Why?"

He had to trot to catch up with the unrelenting youth who answered over his shoulder, "You wouldn't have liked Burdern to go back and find out about his wife and kids, would you? And anyway, Singleton, let's face it, you don't care a duck's fart what happens to either of those two. If killing them could have got you out of the Scrubs, you'd have done the job yourself without a qualm. You may have to do worse to get out of here."

Whitey expected a very furtive and circumspect exit from the college. Instead they found the space around the main gate occupied by a noisy chattering throng of 'Supporters'. Georgie supplied him with a rosette and scarf, saying, "Try to look twenty years younger, eh?"

"How the hell do you do that?"

"Tell yourself there's a big naked blonde just drooling to try you out round every corner."

John Caldercote suddenly appeared at his side. It was a small comfort that he would find it even more difficult to look twenty years younger.

"There you are," he said. "We obviously picked the wrong place to hide, or the wrong time to hide in it."

"Why the hell don't we get out?" demanded Whitey.

"There's safety in numbers," said John. "Or more important, there's normality in numbers. You don't wander round in ones and twos in Oxford; you'd have some other assoles down on you in a flash."

"That's another thing. If the Management knows the Underground are using Jesus, why don't they just tell the assoles and let them sort us out?"

Caldercote smiled superiorly. Whitey sensed that he hadn't had much chance of feeling superior since his arrival here.

"This is a First Team job, one for the professionals, not just a gang of infant Supporters. In fact, if you ask me, a lot of genuine assoles are going to have a pretty rough time of it. I mean, how do you tell the difference?"

He motioned towards the mob that surrounded them.

"And in addition the Management's attitude towards assoles is pretty ambivalent. Publicly they have to be recognized as the good Supporters they are. But they go a bit too far, are a bit too well organized. A lot of people, including your ordinary Supporter, wouldn't mind seeing them roughed up a bit."

"But if there's only a couple of hundred Strikers coming, they wouldn't dare antagonize all the colleges, would they? They'd be outnumbered by twenty to one."

John looked at him curiously.

"You've been away a long time, Whitey," he said finally.

"The First Team play it even harder now than in your day. It's not just a question of numbers."

Something seemed to be happening by the gate. There was as much noise as ever, but over it all now was an air of expectancy and the mob seemed to have sorted itself out into a series of ranks.

"We're off," said John. "Stick close to King."

Now the great gate creaked open and they spilled out of Jesus into the Turl. Someone started chanting 'Onward, Red Supporters' and soon everyone took up the tune as they turned left and with linked arms in strict formation started towards the Broad at a bouncy trot. Beside him Whitey heard John singing as loud as the others, and after a few yards he himself began to join in.

It was an unexpectedly exhilarating experience.

The physical contact, the rhythmic movement, the insistent chants, all combined to give a sense of belonging to an irresistibly powerful group. Other pedestrians in the narrow street, whether assoles or ordinary citizens, ducked into doorways or fled before their trampling advance. Whitey found himself starting to think that such a force as this could build up a momentum which would carry all before it and bring the Management tumbling down. Only the thought that this communal excitement was in fact the main strength of the Four Clubs sobered him slightly, though it was not strong enough to interrupt completely the surges of exhilaration running through his body.

Then they were at the end of the Turl where it joined the Broad, and suddenly the momentum slackened, the chanting died and the irresistible force became an uncertain and fearful throng of seventy or eighty youngsters.

"Oh, shit!" said John.

Two trucks were parked in the middle of the Broad, their bonnets facing Balliol. Out of one of them spilled a line of about twenty men, carrying guns and wearing a uniform which resembled a tightly fitting red track-suit with a broad black line down the sleeves and legs. On their heads they wore snug fitting riot-helmets. Most sinister of all were their red-tinted goggles from which depended small nose and mouth masks clipped tight beneath the chin.

With a smooth precision, which bore the same

relation to the recent movement of the Jays as that of a *corps de ballet* to an Indian war-dance, they ran out into two sides of a triangle, the base of which was the end of the Turl and the apex the second truck. Now the tail-board of this fell slowly away and Whitey found himself staring in disbelief at the menacing snout of a huge cannon.

Nixon Lectures : Fifth Series

Documentary Material
5 (b) Transcript of Rex v Woodcock and others
March 1985 Extract from Mr. Justice
Lauriston's summing up.

The physical and mental suffering you caused this woman is immeasurable. Your only defence, if so it can be styled, seems to be that she was opposed to the demonstration in which you were taking part and that no-one was willing or able to stop you. For *ius civile Britannicorum,* the law of this country, you have substituted *ius virium,* the law of the stronger. Let us then meet you on your own terms. The law of the country permits me to sentence you to a maximum of a mere twenty years on each of the three charges against you. Normally sentences would run concurrently, but on this occasion I too will bring into action *ius virium,* the law of strength.

It is the sentence of this court that each of you shall on each and every count on which you have been found guilty serve a total of not less than twenty years in one of Her Majesty's Penal Institutions.

The sentences will run consecutively.

Chapter 8

Whitey's first thought was that the Strikers were going to lob a few h.e. shells into the Turl. So much for subtlety!

"Fire!" he heard a distant voice command.

And the cannon spoke.

Amazingly it didn't say 'bang!' or any of the normal things a cannon is expected to say. Instead it let out a kind of 'shushing' noise and a great arc of glittering liquid fountained out of it and rained down on the men crowded together at the end of the Turl. Whitey felt himself soaked within seconds, but huge relief was blossoming in his mind. A water-cannon! Who minded getting wet? Perhaps the Team didn't realize how well-armed the Jays were.

As suddenly as it had started the cannon stopped and the Strikers opened fire. Again, not the expected chatter of sub-machineguns but a duller less regular series of explosions.

"What?" he began.

"Gas!" John interrupted, then his eyes grew wide. "For Godsake, Whitey!"

The two men started in wonderment at each other, then looked round at the others.

They were all turning purple.

For a moment Whitey wondered if this were

some hideous side-effect of poison gas.

"The water-cannon!" exclaimed John and began to cry.

Around them the Jays were breaking up in disorder. Many of them had drawn their concealed weapons, but the end of the street was now almost completely obscured in the swirling grey mist of some form of tear-gas whose stinging fumes finished the job of blinding would-be shooters. Entirely disorganized, they began to flee back down the Turl pursued by the swirling gas, like a mob of purple devils in flight from the gates of hell.

Whitey had already begun to recognize the truth of Dr. Johnson's assertion that the imminence of hanging concentrates the mind wonderfully. His own mind had become much attuned to survival in the recent past and even now as he sprinted in as great a panic as any of his companions, his thoughts were busy with the whys and wherefores of his present situation.

Why the purple? Why the gas?

Answers came easily, though not comfortingly. The purple was a means of identification. There was going to be no simple evasive mingling with other groups of assoles. It probably also meant the Management wanted as many as possible alive. Hence the gas. The Strikers in the Broad were mere beaters, driving them in panic and physical distress down the Turl towards . . . well, what did beaters drive the game towards? The waiting guns, the open trap.

Ahead, those Jays who had attempted to turn off the Turl into Ship Street were being driven out by fresh waves of gas. All the exits must be blocked. Whitey stopped running and moved sideways into a shop doorway, pulling Caldercote with him. He dimly recollected this had once been some kind of restaurant but now, in common with so many businesses, it was boarded and barricaded and looked completely impenetrable.

Beside him John shrieked, stumbled and fell as a gas cannister caught him a glancing blow on the shoulder. Whitey stopped and bent to help him up, receiving a huge lung-searing mouthful of fumes as he did so. Choking, he staggered back with John almost a dead weight against him. Behind him, the door gave. He fell backwards, felt himself dragged inside, and lay on the floor, his eyes blinded by tears, and coughing almost to the point of vomiting.

"Quiet!" commanded a familiar voice with such cold urgency in it that he found himself biting deep into his lower lip in an effort to obey.

When his eyesight recovered sufficiently for objects once more to become visible, he saw King crouched by the door, gun in hand, listening attentively.

Whitey put out his hand to push himself upright and came in contact with a recumbent body. His first thought was that it must be Caldercote but when he stood up and looked down at it, he saw an entirely unfamiliar old man. His eyes were open and across the crown of his high-domed bald head ran a jag of blood whose source was a ragged wound on his temple.

King spoke.

"You've got a nicely developed survival bump, Mr. Singleton. I think we can be mutually useful."

He stood up now and came down the narrow passageway, stepping carefully over the old man.

"Those wankers have gone by, but I think we'd better look for a back way out all the same."

"Who's he?" asked Whitey nodding downwards.

"Lives here, I suppose. Or squats here. I had to yuss him. He didn't seem welcoming."

"Where's John? Caldercote, I mean?"

King shrugged.

"They've picked him up I expect. There wasn't time to drag him in. Anyway, he would just have been a drag. Joke. A soft journalist. Too much stodge in his diet and his writing."

"You said as much about mine," said Whitey.

"I don't take it back. But, like I said, you do seem able to survive. I presume you worked out that they'd be waiting in the High?"

"Yes," said Whitey wearily.

"Nice. Let's go."

King headed into the rear of the restaurant. Whitey hesitated, glancing back at the door. Perhaps John was still lying outside there? No. King was right. They'd have picked him up. It wasn't worth the risk of looking.

Everyone I have contact with seems to come

to a sudden end, he thought. Nancy Mays, Burdern, Sheldrake. Now John.

Perhaps I can do as much for King.

With a slight lightening of heart, he went in pursuit of the young terrorist.

Getting out of the building proved easy. A bit of wallclimbing soon had them behind the shops in the Cornmarket which ran parallel to the Turl. But this, Whitey realized, was where their troubles really began.

He had found a tap in the restaurant and paused momentarily to scrub his stained hands.

"A waste of time," grunted King. "It'll take more than water."

He had been right. In any case, it wasn't his hands he should have been worried about. He caught a glimpse of himself in a glass-plated door of a kitchen cabinet and his head looked as if someone had squeezed a muslin bag full of brambles over it.

King also was spattered but nothing like the same extent. Whitey guessd that he must have worked out the cannon function ten seconds ahead of everybody else and grabbed whatever cover was available — probably his nearest companion. But he was still badly enough marked to be easily spotted by any searching Striker.

They crouched low in a jungle of cardboard boxes all packed with old shop rubbish. Some effort had been made at orderly arrangement and most of the rubbish was the kind of packing material one would expect from a clothing store rather than vegetable or other decayable matter. But there was still a strong stench of the rubbish tip about the yard and every whisper of wind among the boxes set Whitey's mind thinking of rats.

Despite this he had no strong urge to leave the yard in his present colourful condition.

"Won't we be safe here till dark?" he asked King. "They can't have any idea how many of you there were. Surely they won't do a house to house search just on the chance of a few stragglers?"

"Why not? It's all in the game, isn't it? Anyway, don't you kid yourself. If we were just a couple of the lads, you might be right. But we're not. We've got names and roles that they'll yuss out of someone in half-an-hour. So they'll be looking for us special. Someone will probably find that old reffer back there pretty soon too. You hide up here if you like. Me, I'm going on."

Whitey was persuaded and followed King forward without further words.

The back of the shop at first sight seemed impenetrable. The windows were boarded up and the single door presented a smooth solid face to the yard, uninterrupted even by handle or key-hole. Obviously no-one was ever expected to make a legitimate entry by this route.

The first floor windows looked more promising. Two weren't shuttered, and of these one even had a small upper casement ajar.

"Can you climb?" asked King.

"If the incentive's right," said Whitey.

The answer was bold, but he recognized that his sadly ill-used body was nearing a point beyond reaction to even the strongest incentive. He looked up at the sun. Late afternoon. Could it possibly still be only yesterday that he had been sitting in the Jap-Line airbus on his way to the Sudan?

"Come on!" hissed King.

Using the boards hammered across the lower windows as a rough ladder, he was now some fifteen feet off the ground and had a handhold on the first floor windowsill.

Whitey joined him, exercising a great deal of care, partly because of his own weakened state and partly because the planks on which they were both standing seemed very resentful of this unexpected weight.

"Grab the sill," ordered King. Whitey obeyed and without further ado King began to scramble upwards, using Whitey's body indiscriminately for toe and knee-holds.

Once on the sill, he hooked one arm through the open casement and reached the other hand down to Whitey.

It was as well he did. Suddenly Whitey felt the board he was standing on begin to give. His grip on the sill was nowhere near strong enough to support him for more than a couple of seconds. Panic-stricken, he flailed out with his left hand, felt King grasp his wrist, felt also the board slip away from beneath his feet and heard it clatter into the yard below. Then with unsuspected strength, the frail figure of King drew him upwards till he was able to get a leg athwart the narrow sill and contribute once more to his own support.

As soon as he saw Whitey was all right, King released him, leaned through the small casement and unlatched the main window. He jumped through and pulled Whitey after him.

They found themselves in a small stock room. Whitey saw he had been right and that it was a clothes shop they had entered. Stiffly he rose to his feet and began to investigate.

King meanwhile had moved to the door where he crouched, gun in hand, listening intently.

"We're in . . ." began Whitey excitedly but tailed off as King hushed him to silence with a viciousness he had not believed a 'shush!' could contain. The youth beckoned him closer and whispered in his ear.

"They've probably got a Sec-man," he said. "If someone heard that plank fall . . ."

He didn't need to say more. Most sizeable shops now employed a Sec-man to stand by the main entrance and watch for trouble. It was a popular employment with ex-Strikers.

"Do you hear anything?" whispered Whitey.

"No."

"Perhaps they're closed?"

"Possibly. With the First Team about, there won't be many people shopping. OK. Let's give it a try."

"Hang on," said Whitey. "We're in luck."

He went to a rack of new coats standing against a wall, picked one of the right size and put it on. It was of an antique style and cut compared with the American clothing he had become used to, but it provided an excellent cover for the purple-splashed brown suit he had borrowed from John Caldercote.

King nodded approval and joined him, quickly making his choice. They were mostly in shades of Athletic red, but to Whitey's surprise King followed his own example and chose a light brown shade, one of the few non-significant colours left since red, blue, green and yellow had been appropriated by the Four Clubs. He put his gun down to get his arms through the sleeves which were rather narrow. At precisely the moment when both his hands were jammed halfway down their respective sleeves, the door opened.

It was a woman. She opened her mouth to scream as she spotted them, but the shock of their appearance, particularly the monstrous purple of most of Whitey's face, constricted her throat just too long, and Whitey's fingers were there, redoubling the pressure.

"Not a word," he snarled, dragging her into the room and shutting the door. "Not a word or you're dead!"

He was not going to repeat his error of over-gentleness with Nancy. King raised his eyebrows at him, smiling slightly, and finished putting on his coat.

"Better," he said looking down at himself. "It's a pity masks aren't in fashion, though."

"Hang on," said Whitey. He turned to the terrified woman and started going through the pockets of the red over-all she was wearing, finding what he wanted almost instantly. Triumphantly he held it up. Again an anachronism in American terms, but still to be found in plenty over here.

A powder compact.

When he'd finished using it, he and King still looked distinctly odd, but it was a different kind of oddness from being purple-faced.

"We might pass for a couple of glibs," said Whitey.

"Or reluctant lepers," said King, examining himself in the compact mirror. "Now all we want are hats to cover our bonny purple hair."

The woman suddenly made a move and the gun was in King's hand in an instant. But she ignored it, pulling open a drawer to reveal an assortment of Athletic headgear.

"Thanks," said King choosing a floppy cap, while Whitey opted for a kind of woollen nightcap which he pulled down over his ears, thus affording him maximum coverage.

"Doesn't he look nice," said King to the woman who obediently turned to look at Whitey. The barrel of the gun took her just above the ear and she fell senseless with hardly a noise.

"Why the hell did you do that?" demanded Whitey furiously. "She was helping us."

111

"With the hats? No. That was just reaction. She'd realized we weren't going to rape her. They're always so relieved when they realize that, haven't you noticed? But she'd have shrieked her head off the minute we left. Come on!"

The storeroom door opened on to a small alcove at the back of the first floor sales area. There was no-one in sight. King had been right. The presence of the First Team in town sent people heading for home. Even good local Supporters knew better than to risk being yussed by accident.

Downstairs Whitey realized King had been right again. A Sec-man stood by the door, complete with black crash-helmet and truncheon. Worse, he was chatting with a couple of First Team Strikers. Obviously he was a retired member himself and they were discussing common acquaintances. Happily the shop was not too brightly lit and they were able to pause unseen on a small landing till the Strikers went on their way, though their farewell exchange, spoken in rather louder voices as they moved off, was not very comforting.

"Watch out for any of these wankers," said one of the men.

"And we want them alive," warned the other; rather spoiling things by adding, "So they can talk, that is; not necessarily so they can walk!"

They disappeared and King murmured, "No point in waiting. He's not going anywhere."

Swiftly they descended the remaining stairs. Whitey caught a glimpse of himself in a full length mirror as they crossed the shop floor and his heart sank. Even if the Sec-man decided he just hadn't noticed these two customers enter (unlikely, in the case of a well-trained forward as this one seemed to be) he would have to be half blind and totally incurious not to take note of their exiting.

He was neither half-blind nor totally incurious and he stood across the door as they approached, effectively blocking their exit.

"Excuse me," said King. "Do you own a car?"

The question clearly surprised the Sec-man as much as it did Whitey. His hand which had been moving easily down to his truncheon paused now.

"What?" he said. "Yes."

"That's good. We'd like to borrow it. Is it parked close?"

As he spoke King took his hand out of his pocket for a moment and showed the man his gun. The man licked his lips, more pensively than in fear, and looked from King to Whitey who had the wit to thrust his own right hand deeper into his newly stolen coat's pocket and make a menacing movement.

"Let's go find it, shall we?" said King. "Nice and easy now. Nothing sudden. We don't want to have to take your name."

A good Striker knows when to drop back in defence, as the proverb says, and the Sec-man turned without argument and led them into the almost deserted street. They walked for half a minute toward the Martyrs' Memorial. As they approached it, King said conversationally, "If we don't reach your car in another thirty seconds, there's going to be another martyr."

They were at it in fifteen.

"Keys," said King. As the Sec-man handed them over, Whitey wondered gloomily what they were going to do with him. He had less objection to King's method of disposal in this case, but the wide open spaces of the Corn with a couple of red-suited Strikers still visible in the distance was not the best of places to flatten somebody.

Suddenly the Sec-man arranged things for them. He did it all by the book. The keys slipped through his fingers. King involuntarily stooped to catch them, the truncheon leapt into the Sec-man's hand and flailed round against the top of Whitey's right arm with numbing force. If he had been grasping a gun in his pocket, he wouldn't have been able to use it, which was of course the Sec-man's intention. It was certainly all very much by the book, but it killed the Sec-man. For Whitey had no gun, so could have been ignored. And King was of first team quality in a higher league than any known to the Sec-man. His move for the keys had been but the shadow of a reflex, just enough to anger him at his own weakness, and the gun in his pocket had spoken twice before the truncheon could be cocked for a second blow.

Whitey thought he had become used to pain but discovered that it takes a lot to wear the fine edge off a man's appreciation. He staggered against the car, clutching his arm and once more had to be dragged to safety by King, who was already inside.

The reason for his haste quickly became clear. The two distant Strikers had turned, even at a distance of a quartermile recognizing the report of King's gun. Now they were sprinting towards them, whistles blowing, and even as King flung the car into a tyre-rending U-turn and headed north, a pursuit vehicle came nosing out of the Broad to rendezvous briefly with the two Strikers, then take up the chase.

For the next half-hour Whitey stopped thinking. At first he stared in terror out of the rear window, then in even greater terror out of the front. King was bent on thrusting the road into the car's bonnet like an Italian eating spaghetti. Finally he closed his eyes and let his mind go blank.

Even then some impressions of the chase forced themselves in. The pursuit vehicle had the greater speed, but King knew the roads better. He had very rapidly turned off the main Banbury Road and squeezed the car violently down a series of minor roads twisting and turning, but always ultimately getting the declining sun shining through the passenger window. Whitey needed the warmth, but did not suspect his chauffeur of mere solicitude. They were making north and when after forty-five minutes of this nightmarish journey, the car slowed down to a pleasantly sedate pace he did not need the explanation his companion offered him.

"They won't follow us here," said King with a laugh. "We've crossed the line. We're in Wanderers territory now."

It was a small enough relief. One danger had merely been exchanged for a lesser. But Whitey felt as relieved as a drowning man hauled into a leaking boat. Anything was better than nothing.

Also he now had time to feel very ill.

Nixon Lectures: Fifth Series

Audio-Visual Material
1 (m) Extract from tape of Reith Lecture No. 4 (The Law is An Ass) 1984, given by Professor Arthur Drake, Department of Social Studies, Coventry University.

Hitherto my approach has been historical. I have tried to trace the serpentine path by which our modern concept of the law has moved from the Mosaic to the Democratic. I have tried to show how law as the voice of god was turned by an act of political ventriloquism into law as the voice of the people. And I have tried to look objectively at the often violent and bloody means whereby in our own century, this deception has been unmasked.

But objectivity itself is a concept under heavy philosophical challenge. Like the concept of the rule of law, that last resort of desperate politicians in the sixties and seventies, objectivity must be viewed with grave suspicion. It goes hand in hand with that other old favourite, rationality, though a rationality which somehow arrives at the conclusion that all men are equal is hardly objective. And when it fails to recognize the absurdity of having laws to enforce this alleged equality, it becomes itself merely absurd.

And a rationality which expects men to submit to laws laid down by other men in other times for other purposes is more than absurd. It is irrational.

The Trade Unions are showing us the way. First by opposing management, then by opposing government and finally and most significantly by opposing and destroying their own controlling bodies.

At last we are on the verge of a free society where man's individual voice can once more be heard and where the old anodyne of the single vote is rejected with scorn! So-called objectivity and rationality have been the chains by which we have been bound to a dying civilization.

Thank God we are shaking them off! Thank God all the old stupid petty reffing rules and restrictions are being revealed as the crap they are, crap we've been wallowing in for centuries.

Thank God, or thank the Lord of the reffing Flies for that matter, that we're getting a glimpse of a world where men can be themselves and speak what they mean not what they ought to say.

I work in a University and I tell you this, friends; our universities and colleges are full of crap-merchants, sterile minds, streaks of old dried dung, men with their eyes in their arseholes and their brains in a specimen bottle, oh I could name names, taking years to do reff all in the name of rational thought or objective research. Thank Christ it'll soon be over and we can spew the wankers out, yes, I can see it coming and this little shit of a producer what the hell are you waving your arms for you stupid prick why don't you

End of tape.

Chapter 9

For the next three days Whitey left himself completely in the care of King. How or where the youth made contact with the local Jays he did not know. In his waking moments he was quite lucid, but felt quite incapable either physically or mentally of making any self-originated effort. He accepted without question the shelter, food and medication given him. Even when a very presentable young woman, bikini-clad, led him into a shower and began coating him with some oily substance which under the stinging jets carried away the purple dye, it was not until she turned her attention from his head to those spots where the dye had soaked through to his body, that he began to react.

"Feeling better?" she asked amiably. But that was as far as it went. He returned to his bed and spent a restless, uncomfortable night, from which surprisingly he awoke feeling much more like his old self.

"Feeling better," repeated King when he arrived with a breakfast tray next morning. He made it a statement, not a question.

"Where are we?" asked Whitey. "And why are you taking such good care of someone you consider as worthless as me?"

"You *are* feeling better," said King. He had obtained for himself a rather smart cat-suit in Wanderers blue with a white buckskin fringe down the sleeves and round the ankles. His pale, round face, smiling now, looked even younger than the nineteen or twenty years Whitey had estimated.

"It's much the same set-up as at Oxford," he said. "This time we're on the old Coventry University campus. It's a historical place this in a way. At most of the Universities and Colleges in the country when the dissolution started there was a strong body of student resistance. Sheffield for instance was almost completely gutted in the ensuing struggle. But here the students unanimously passed a resolution welcoming the move, hurled out all the teaching and admin staff who were less than one hundred per cent enthusiastic, and re-constituted themselves as a Supporters Club."

"Tell *me* something I don't know," said Whitey waspishly. "I was alive and well and working for my living when all this happened. But how did your lot get a footing here?"

"Easy. Even in those dim and distant days when you were alive and well and working, there were people here who were very anti, but went along for the ride. Because there was no fight, they were never weeded out. They passed the torch on. As you'll know, being so old and knowledgeable, people generally move out of these residential Clubs in their mid-twenties. Get married, work for a living, that sort of thing. This suits us well. We recruit from the new intake of young Supporters. Very carefully. Very slowly. We have their active support and help while they're at their fittest, physically and mentally — late teens, early twenties. Then off they go and become norms. Waiting for the day."

"I know," said Whitey cynically. "The cemeteries of the world are full of people who died of old age waiting for the day."

"We haven't been going that long," observed King. "Your generation was all wind and words. It's only in the last half dozen years that the ball's really started rolling."

"That's more like it!" said Whitey. He pushed aside the breakfast tray whose contents he had been enthusiastically wolfing down while King talked, clambered out of bed and explored his body with the seismometer of his mind. The tremors of pain were still there, but distant now and receding further and further into the deep core.

"More like what?"

"Like the attitude I expect from you. You've avoided the second part of my question. Why are you looking after me so well?"

He looked round the room for his clothes. There was no sign of the overlarge, purple-stained suit he had borrowed from poor John Caldercote, but draped over the back of King's chair were a pair of slacks and a blue tunic-shirt. Someone had been most thoughtful. He began to pull them on.

"Perhaps," said King slowly, with a faint smile which made him look no more than fifteen, "perhaps deep down we're not revolutionaries at all, merely conservative old hoarders. We hate to throw anything away. You never know; one day it might come in useful."

"Fine," said Whitey. "It's nice to know you're so well motivated. Will this benevolence extend to getting me out of the country?"

"I shouldn't think so," said King, quite serious now. "You know a lot about us. Away from our care and protection, you'd be very vulnerable."

"You don't mean the Clubs are organized internationally?" interjected Whitey in disbelief.

"Hardly," answered King. "Something as parochial as this would find that very hard. But there are those who sympathize. In any case, it's not just outside pressures that are dangerous. As a journalist, I'm sure you'd find it hard not to drop knowledgeable hints about your exciting adventures in Old England. No, you're better off here."

"Waiting for the day?"

"It may come sooner than you think."

"Promises, promises," said Whitey gloomily. "You don't really mean that some kind of uprising's just round the corner, do you? No, don't bother to tell me. It seems the less I know, the better off I'll be. Look, can I go out of this place, or do I stay cooped up in here for ever?"

King thought a moment.

"Wait," he said, and left the room.

Gone to check, thought Whitey almost glee-fully. The King too must obey.

He looked at himself in the wall-mirror. Be-neath the tan he had collected from his recent stay in the East, his face was drawn and blood-less. In his casual tunic and slacks, he might have been a sick man trying to regain his strength on a convalescent holiday. But he knew that outside this building the blue of his tunic would tell the onlooker that he was something quite different. A friend, an ally, a Supporter. And fifty miles south it would tell yet another story.

King came back in and tossed Whitey a blue and white cardboard kepi and rosette.

"Camouflage," he said. "It should do. You don't look much like the *Nuspic* photo and that's all the Strikers will have if they're out looking for you."

"You think that's likely here?" he asked, pin-ning the rosette high on his left shoulder.

"On the thigh," said King. "Here they're wear-ing them on the left thigh. You never know what's likely. Sometimes I think there's a much greater degree of co-operation between the top management than the ordinary Supporter would dream of. Come on. I'll show you round."

The Coventry campus had the same air of neglect and decay which marked all large centres of population. Here there were comparatively few traces of the aftermath of battle, or even of the Supporters' formation marches which could leave a trail of destruction several miles long.

124

Such expressions of enthusiasm for the Club they saved up until their own living quarters were safely behind. But maintenance was a different matter. No norm was going to be foolish enough to come on campus to work, and the internal organization did not go far beyond keeping essential power supplies going. Time too leads a destructive march and Whitey had to tread carefully over cracked paving stones through which had pushed vigorous weeds sown on the wind which blew across the neglected lawns and fields of the University. The towering blocks, whose ground floors were often almost obscured by piles of uncollected rubbish, were patterned with cracked window-panes; and broken pipes sent water spluttering athwart the walls whose tiled fascia had come adrift in places so that the buildings looked as if they were suffering from a kind of architectural leprosy.

In the middle of a paved courtyard, at what only an optimistic fireman would have called a safe distance from the buildings, a great fire glowed and from time to time in a fashion more desultory than purposeful, figures approached it clutching boxes full of rubbish which they hurled on. The air was full of smoke and charred paper.

"What are they doing?" Whitey asked. "Burning books?"

"You're too romantic," observed King. "Your Englishman's never feared books like most other Europeans. Occasionally they may be a moral danger but never a political one. No, it's just a

125

way of keeping the level of rubbish below the first floor windows. And it's something to do between demonstrations."

"Yes, that's been puzzling me," said Whitey. "What in fact do they do? I expected to see more of them around."

"There are still classes going on. Tactical discussions. Club history. That sort of thing. It's even possible, if you play the ball right and have a good line in Supporters' jargon, to get something like an old-time university education."

"It's nice to think the place is still full of classical scholars," observed Whitey. "What does the Management think about these places? They must know the Underground's very active in them."

"Of course. But what can they do? In Oxford it was easier for them as we were concentrated in a single college. That was almost an accident. We just gradually took the place over! Here, everybody's spread right across the campus. No single one of us knows more than half a dozen others. We've been infiltrated, naturally. But then we've infiltrated the infiltrators, so a lot of misleading information's been fed back."

He laughed freely.

"In fact if the First Team ever do come in here to mop up, a lot of very good Supporters are going to find themselves on the penalty spot!"

Whitey shuddered. His next planned article on the state of Britain was going to need a lot of revision. If he ever got the chance to write it.

"Well," he said as lightly as he could manage, "I'll be very careful who I talk to."

King looked at him with an enigmatic half-smile.

"Don't worry," he said. "We'll take care of you. We'll see you don't get captured."

They walked on in silence. A couple of Supporters overtook them, shouting a greeting. Whitey opened his mouth to answer, realized he was about to call, "Preds!" and bit it back. Up here the greeting was "Blest!" "Preds" would be the ultimate insult.

The two Supporters were heading towards a large semi-ovoid structure which seemed to be made of some grey fabric rather than concrete, brick, or stone. It looked like a flat-bottomed airship, resting on the ground.

"What's that?"

"That? The inflatable building you mean? It's been there for years, I believe. No-one remember why it was erected. But the Disciplinary Committee use it now. There must be a Hearing on. Like to take a look?"

Whitey nodded and they went into the building together, having to pass through an air-lock to avoid deflating the structure.

Inside they found a huge press of Supporters and it was quite impossible to see what was going on.

"Must be something good," murmured King. "Not just a normal internal Hearing."

He poked the nearest Supporter in the ribs.

"What's the score, friend?" he asked.

"Psycho-yuss," answered the other gleefully. "Two periods of extra time so far! But the speakers have gone bust. They're fixing them now."

King whistled.

"That means they've been at it ten hours," he whispered.

"At what?"

"Some poor reffer's being persuaded to make a public confession of his crimes against the Club."

"You mean they're torturing somebody in here?" demanded Whitey indignantly.

"Not with hot pincers, if that's what you mean. It's all done by questioning. Let's get a bit nearer."

At that moment someone started a chant which at its second syllable was taken up by everyone in the building so that even the sound-absorbent walls were forced to give back a dull echo of the sound.

"United SHIT! Athletic SHIT! Rovers SHIT!"

Whitey felt a sharp elbow dig him in the ribs and, looking at King, he saw that his companion was joining in the shout with apparent enthusiasm. Quickly he began chanting too. It went on for several minutes with undiminished vigour and then the chant modulated into the chorus of the Wanderers song. Whitey did not know the words but he bellowed approximations in his loudest hoarsest voice.

As the final notes died away, King murmured, "Don't overdo it."

Whitey saw that a couple of nearby Supporters were giving him puzzled looks. He had to remind himself again that these were not the straightforward brutish thugs their costume and behaviour indicated, but highly intelligent youths.

There was some relaxation in the crowd ahead as about fifty of the lads began to force their way out. From their conversation, it appeared that they had some special Riot planned for that afternoon, though they seemed rather disappointed at having to leave the game before the end.

King moved rapidly forward before those in front could rejoin in their inpenetrably tight ranks. Whitey followed, ignoring the protests that went up, until one particularly large youth swung round threateningly and demanded, "You for goal, friend?" This seemed to have some ritual significance and heads turned to take in the situation. For all Whitey knew, there was a ritual reply. King was too far ahead to help. The best he could manage was to shake his head and mutter, "No offence."

Whether this would have sufficed was not tested as a loud metallic voice suddenly boomed through the air, saying, "That's fixed it," and a great cheer went up, diverting everyone's attention.

Whitey managed to put another couple of bodies between himself and his threatener before being brought to a final halt by sheer density of numbers. But he had at last reached a position where he could see something of what was going on in the centre of the hall.

There was a raised platform, bearing a table behind which sat half a dozen Supporters. These he presumed were the Disciplinary Committee. About twenty feet in front of them standing on a small round podium was a slight figure who looked to be in the last stages of exhaustion. Its hunched, dejected posture made it difficult to tell whether it was a youth or a girl, and the Wanderers blue tunic and slacks gave no clue.

A couple of yards behind the podium stood a double rank of about a dozen Strikers. Whitey assumed they were local products rather than members of the Wanderers First Team, but they looked a formidable lot in their blue track-suits. They had truncheons hanging at their sides but no automatic weapons and this confirmed Whitey's guess. Only genuine First Team Strikers were allowed to carry arms.

"Sorry, friends, but it's all fixed now," said one of the platform figures into a microphone. "As Chairman, I declare this Hearing of the Disciplinary Committee to be resumed."

Another cheer went up and the crowd swayed gently in unison. They were prevented from encroaching on the central area by an encirclement of linked crash barriers, one of several types used in the last days of the old football matches in an attempt to preserve order on the terraces by barricading rival factions from each other. They had been strong enough to succeed, but in the end proved only another cause of escalation as the missile boys took over, hurling stones, bottles, darts, anything they could find, into the neighbouring pen. And finally came the showers of acid and the Molotov cocktails.

"Now, Our Friend," said the Chairman in a kind voice, using the traditional form of address to anyone called before the Committee, "we are ready to resume the discussion. Is there anything you would like to say at this point?"

The accused murmured something which even the neckmike could not pick up. The Chairman made a sign and one of the Strikers stepped forward with a glass of water which he gave to the accused who drank.

"There now, Friend," said the Chairman, still sounding like a benevolent uncle. "What did you say?"

"Please," the voice was now audible, but low and strained, "Please, I'm very tired, I should like to sit down."

The Chairman did not answer for a moment, but looked at his fellow committee members.

"So," he said finally. "You would like to sit down. Look around you, Our Friend. Go on, look around you!"

Slowly the accused's head rose and slowly began to turn. It was a girl. The face was expressionless, not through the exertion of self-control but because fatigue had drained all feeling from the brain behind it. The eyes stared blankly, unseeingly, into the crowd. Whitey felt their gaze pass slowly over his face and ducked his head instinctively though he knew that nothing was being registered. When he raised it again the girl had resumed her posture of anonymous dejection. But there was no doubt about her identity in Whitey's mind.

It was Hydrangea, the girl from the plane.

"What do you see, Friend," asked the Chairman, and now his voice began to rise and a hysterically angry note began to replace the avuncular kindliness.

"What do you see? I'll tell you what you see. You see good, honest, loyal Supporters, come here today to see that this Hearing is fair, come here today to share in your examination, come here today to give you their support! That's what you see! And are they sitting? Are *they* sitting? No. You see they are not. And do they complain? Do they ask for chairs? No, they do not!

"Yet *you,* the central cause, the only reason why these hundreds of good, loyal Supporters have to spend hours standing and waiting, *you* want a chair! *you want a chair!*"

He collapsed back in his seat as though his outburst had exhausted him.

The crowd burst into applause, clapping their hands above their heads (the only possible way of doing it) and swaying more violently than before.

The Chairman spoke again.

"We have treated you well. Perhaps too well.

132

We have given you every chance to explain yourself. Perhaps it's time we saw you in your true colours. Whatever they are."

He snapped his fingers. Two Strikers moved forward holding in their upraised arms a selection of garments in Athletic red, United yellow and City green. A great growling roar of disapproval went up from the crowd, turning into a cheer as the Strikers hurled them down in disgust before the girl.

"Help yourself," said the Chairman. "Pick whichever you please. Pick the colours which belong to you."

The girl looked up.

"No," she said. "I'm wearing my colours. Please, these are my colours, I'm a good Supporter."

She did not sound as if she believed herself. The Chairman flung up his arms in disgust.

"Must we do it for you?" he cried. "Right. If you force us, we will."

The two Strikers returned, seized Hydrangea's tunic and began literally tearing it off her back. She did not resist and in a few seconds was stripped to her underclothes. The crowd roared in approval as the Strikers then began to dress her. Green trousers, yellow jacket, and finally they rammed a bright red beret on to her head. She made no effort to resist but stood as they left her, half turned round to face the crowd, like a grotesque and defeated Harlequin.

"Face the Committee, Friend," said the Chairman when the noise had died away. Slowly she shuffled round.

"Now what have you to say?" he demanded. "Now we see you as you are."

"I appeal to the Management," she said slowly and with great effort. "I want a fair trial."

"The Management? Why should the Management waste time on you? And what do you mean by 'trial'? This is no trial, Our Friend. A trial establishes guilt or innocence. There is no such doubt here. Our labours are all for your benefit. Do you think we derive pleasure from seeing you in those abhorrent colours? No, we do not. We want to help you to be able to wear the one, the only, the *True* Blue once more. You have been obdurate but we have been patient. We have followed you round the circle of your deceptions seeking a way in. You say you have been a Supporter all your life, yet you cannot sing more than the first verse of our song. You say you are a native of Birmingham, yet your answers to questions about that city are strangely inaccurate. You say you came to Coventry to join this Supporters Club, yet you entered the campus stealthily and were only detected through the eternal vigilance of one of our Strikers. Why did you come? Where did you come from? Who are you?"

Good questions, thought Whitey. Ones that he himself would very much like to hear answered. But somehow whenever he encountered this girl, she was in a state so parlous that her own responsibility for his troubles became insignificant.

She was speaking again, finding strength from somewhere to raise her voice and almost control the trembling in it.

"I have a right," she began.

"Right? You?" screamed the Chairman. "You have no right even to talk of rights! You think only of yourself, of *your* fatigue, of *your* hunger, *your* rights. We have been here more then ten hours and you have learned nothing!"

An outburst of applause drowned the girl's reply but Whitey, his eyes fixed intently on her lips thought he caught it.

"Nor have you."

Now the crowd launched into the club song and again Whitey was constrained to mouth approximations of the words. As it finished a new cry was started up.

Off! Off! Off! Off!

It was accompanied by the rhythmic waving of one hand held straight up in the air with the index finger pointed.

Off! Off! Off! Off!

Whitey joined in. There was nothing else to do.

Off! Off! Off! Off!

The sound was deafening.

Off! Off! Off! Off!

It went on for more than ten minutes. The Commitee sat perfectly still. The Strikers stood at strict military attention. The girl swayed slightly . . .

. . . and fell.

Instantly the chant eased and the silence which took its place was the more terrifying. Nothing happened for a long moment then the Chairman stood up.

"This Hearing is adjourned," he said.

Two of the Strikers dragged Hydrangea to her feet. The other Strikers went forward and removed a section of the crash barrier. Immediately the crowd spilled forward and the area of open space disappeared in a second.

Slowly the Strikers began to force a way through the still tightly packed throng, closely followed by the two men carrying Hydrangea. The Supporters were now working themselves up into a frenzy of hatred, swearing obscenity at the girl while those who were near enough spat at the still body and aimed blows at it. The surge of bodies suddenly brought King alongside Whitey once more. The young man's face was working with a fury it was difficult not to believe genuine. Whitey seized his arm so they should not be separated.

"What happens now?" he bawled in his ear. There was no danger of being overheard. The din was so tremendous that it was difficult to hear King's reply even though delivered at top volume from a distance of about six inches.

"They take her out. Show her the fire. Terrify the guts out of her. Then she's shoved back inside with just the Committee. No one else.

Complete quiet. Gentle questions. That's when they break."

Hydrangea's still body passed quite close on its way to the door. Whitey thought she might be dead but her eyes flickered open for a moment and seemed to focus on his face. But there was no recognition there.

Then she was carried out of sight through the mob who were now fighting their way out of the exits at such a rate that the air-locks could not function properly and the high dome began to collapse on to its metal frame.

"Not to worry," said King, sensing Whitey's concern. "It always happens."

Still clinging together they made their way outside.

The crowd of Supporters, joined by many others who had not been at the Hearing, now centred on the huge bonfire on which the campus rubbish was burnt. Even at a distance of a hundred metres, its flames were clearly visible above the heads of the spectators and the plume of black smoke which drifted on the wind must have been observable from the centre of the city.

Varied images rose up in Whitey's mind. Red Indian torture, primitive sacrifice, medieval witch-burning. He turned to King again, needing reassurance.

"They won't hurt her? Burn her, I mean?"

"Unlikely. Though they have been carried away in the past. No, the point is to break not destroy. She's done well. Usually an eight or nine hours Hearing itself is enough."

Whitey relaxed his grip on King and began to force himself through the crowd. Something of his emotion must have showed on his face as no-one offered more than a token protest at his brutal pushing.

The inner circle of the crowd had been pushed by the weight of spectators behind closer to the fire than was comfortable. Hydrangea made fully conscious by fear, was contained in a tight pen of Strikers the only gap in which led towards the flames. She pressed herself back against the human wall to escape the heat, but they thrust her away violently towards the edge of the fire, repeating the manoeuvre with increasing force each time she tried to escape. At each thrust, the crowd shrieked rhythmically, like the audience at a bull-fight. The Strikers seemed to be in the grip of a self-induced hypnosis, pushing and waiting, pushing and waiting. Whitey looked desperately around for some sign that there would soon be an end to this, some indication that authority was still present. But the Disciplinary Committee must still be sitting at their table, patiently awaiting the return of their prisoner.

She would never get back, Whitey could see that now. The ring of Strikers had moved slowly forward till now their thrusts were sending her almost into the flames. The emotional blankness had fled from her face and been replaced by desperate, unreasoning fear.

Another thrust. She staggered forward, made

a huge effort to stop short of the flames, and fell. The crowd roared its approval. Slowly she pushed herself upright, the patterning of heat on her face and bare forearms clearly visible. Then she turned to the fire and ran quickly forward. For a second Whitey thought she had decided on self-immolation, but she retreated instantly from the flames.

And when she turned to face the semi-circle of strikers, she held a fiercely burning length of wood in her hand.

For a moment she looked like Defiance personified and the crowd was silenced and moved uneasily backwards. The Strikers too were momentarily taken aback, but quickly recovered, drew their truncheons and spread out to give themselves room for action. Suddenly Hydrangea was just a girl again, ludicrously threatening a thousand men with a stick. The crowd began to laugh and jeer. The sound seemed to get to Hydrangea as nothing the Committee had said had been able to. With a high-pitched scream of terror and fury she flung herself forward, swinging the brand above her head so that a stream of sparks followed close behind.

The Strikers scattered to avoid the onslaught. One tried to counter, swinging a blow with his truncheon at her head, but she ducked beneath it and rammed the burning billet into his face. He fell, screaming.

But success could only be shortlived. The crowd was too densely packed to be scattered by a single-pronged attack and Hydrangea realized it. She halted, swinging the brand round and round to keep the Strikers at a distance. But there was no way out. All they had to do was wait till she tired. Or till the burning stick went out.

Desperately she stared around. Yet again her gaze fell on Whitey. This time he met it full on. And this time incredulous recognition dawned in her eyes.

The Strikers, sensing her distraction, tried to move in, but she countered with wild blows from her weapon. One of the Strikers parried with his truncheon, the stick snapped and the burning end fell to the ground.

Seeing her defenceless the whole crowd surged forward. There seemed to be some alternative activity at the rear which was causing some heads to turn, but those at the front were clearly bent on destroying the girl. With what looked like the last effort of her exhausted frame, she flung herself at Whitey, locked her arms around his neck and sobbed, "Help me. Please help me."

"I can't," he said wretchedly. "I can't."

A Striker seized her shoulders and tried to wrench her clear, but her grip was strong. Whitey knew that at the moment it must appear that she had picked on him purely by chance. He ought to be thrusting her from him, expressing his fury and hate like a good Supporter.

"Watch yourself, friend," said the Striker raising his truncheon above Hydrangea's head. "This'll make the reffing bitch move!"

The blow began to fall, Whitey swung his knee into the man's groin and he doubled up with a shriek compounded of pain and amazement. For a second no one was sure what had happened, but when he swung his fist into the face of the next Striker to approach, all doubt fled.

Whitey sought desperately for something to do, something to say, which could save him. But looking round the ring of murderous faces, he knew that there was no way to stop them killing him.

A man can rarely pick the place of his death, he recalled saying in a sententiously elegiac piece composed during the Formosan war. He certainly would not have chosen, nor even guessed at, this. By a mound of burning garbage on an English University campus.

The Strikers advanced. The crowd seethed, shouted, swayed. And parted.

"Wait," said a voice.

No single voice had the power to stop these men. Not even if the heavens had opened and the voice come from above. But this voice had something very persuasive about it. The something was a squad of First Team Strikers each armed with a hand-gun. Suddenly the local Strikers looked young, gauche boys, their movements uncertain, their track-suits ill-fitting, shoddy cheap imitations of the real thing. There was no chance of confusion. The owner of the voice stepped into the circle of heat round the fire and stared speculatively at Whitey.

It was Chaucer, the Wanderers' Assistant Manager.

"Who's your Captain?" he demanded.

One of the Strikers came awkwardly forward.

"You know me? Good. The Management wants these two. I'll take them now."

"But," protested the Captain, "she's before the Committee, I mean, and this wanker, we don't know who . . ."

"I'll take them," repeated Chaucer.

Whitey waited anxiously for the Captain's response. He had no reason to like Chaucer, but at least he offered an alternative to immediate death. In the crowd held back now by the First Team, he caught a glimpse of King. Perhaps he could arrange something. He had promised, "We won't let you be captured."

The Captain looked round at the row of armed men and came to the only decision.

"Of course, Mr. Chaucer. Blest."

"Blest."

Everyone relaxed visibly. The crowd began chattering among themselves and the First Team moved forward to carve a path through them once more.

Again Whitey glimpsed King, very close now. The crowd opened for a second and he saw that the young Jay was holding something low down, close to his hip. A gun. It was absurd. To try a rescue by frontal assault in these circumstances was suicidal.

Again he remembered the promise. "We won't let you be captured."

And suddenly it no longer sounded like a re-assurance, but a threat. He dropped to the ground with Hydrangea as the gun went off. Something whistled so close to his head he felt its passage. Automatically he put his hand up to seek for damage. It came down red and sticky. He felt ill. Then something fell across him and when he pushed it aside, he saw the source of the blood.

The Captain of the local Strikers had taken the bullet in the throat.

The First Team were among the crowd. There was confusion and panic everywhere.

Someone seized him by the arm. It was Chaucer.

"Come on," he snapped. "It's a good time to go."

Statistical Material
4 (p) Extract from Annual Abstract of Statistics
No. ·121, 1985 published by the Central
Statistical Office of Great Britain.

TABLE 75: *Persons found guilty: Analysis by type
of offence.*
England and Wales.

	1982	1983	1984
Burglary	92,784	96,839	105,206
Fraud	19,458	20,965	24,703
Theft	201,562	203,984	227,654
Handling Stolen Goods	28,983	30,112	34,376
Sexual Offences	8,497	9,003	14,026
Murder	128	163	305
Manslaughter	250	283	464
Wounding	29,782	31,765	36,304
Other Offences Against Person	1,309	1,682	2,306
Other Indictable Offences	14,551	16,209	20,506
Total Indictable Offences	397,304	411,005	465,850
Indictable Offences known to the police	2,268,593	2,598,763	3,446,662

Chapter 10

"You saved my life, I saved yours," said Chaucer. "I stole your clothes, now I give you new ones. The score's level between us."

"Rubbish," answered Whitey made bold by the excellent wine they were drinking. "I took a risk to save your life, you took none to save mine. And in addition, your predicament had nothing to do with me, whereas mine was contributed to indirectly by your theft of my clothes."

He nodded emphatically and refilled his glass. They were sitting at a table which bore the remnants of a superbly cooked and stylishly served meal of a kind whose existence in present day England he would seriously have doubted. The surroundings matched the meal. He had expected to be taken to the local version of the Scrubs. Or at best to Wanderers Heights, the Birmingham equivalent (though, as the PR men never failed to point out, two hundred feet higher) of Athletic House in London.

Instead they had come to this mid-nineteenth century industrialist's manor house, solidly constructed, but fortunately designed by an architect who had not forgotten the Regency's sense of proportion. The furnishings were in perfect harmony with the room and, if genuine, would be worth a fortune anywhere in the world except England, where art and the artist were regarded as suspiciously as they had been in Hitler's Germany or Plato's Republic.

"So you think I still owe you?" asked Chaucer amiably.

Whitey regarded him speculatively. But the motives behind Chaucer's friendliness were too obscure for his wine-clouded brain to work out. In any case he was finding that experience was making a philosopher out of him, a kind of pragmatic, stoic, cynical hedonist. He reached for the decanter again.

"I've got to believe you still owe me," he said. "Once you stop owing me, then it's good-bye to this."

His gesture included the table, the dining room, the comfortable bedroom in which he had changed into his well-cut suit, the whole house with its well defended grounds.

"Perhaps one night of this pays off the score," said Chaucer. He sounded as if he might mean it and Whitey sobered up slightly. It seemed a good subject to change.

"Any news of King?" he asked. He had seen no reason not to answer Chaucer's questions about the course of events which had brought him to Coventry. What happened in Athletic territory could hardly concern him. In any case the Jesuits were scattered — most of them probably captured or dead by now, he thought, remembering the purple dye.

And the presence of subversive cells in the Coventry campus clearly came as no news to Chaucer. Whitey could honestly claim he knew next to nothing. He could not even have found the residential block in which he had been kept with any certainty, and the only people he knew by sight were King and perhaps the pretty girl who'd scrubbed the dye off him.

"No, he got clean away," grunted Chaucer. "Stuck the gun into some poor reffer's hand then just faded into the crowd. My Strikers got the fellow holding the gun, of course. Took them two hours to realize their mistake."

"What then? Apologize, pat him on the back and let him go?" asked Whitey ironically.

"What? There's not much to let go after two hours with the First Team," said Chaucer. "Interesting little wanker he sounds, this King. What I really want to know is why he took such a risk just to try to silence you."

"Obvious. Because I could identify him," answered Whitey triumphantly, but aware even as he spoke of the flaw in his reasoning.

"Shooting off a gun with twenty Strikers a few yards away is as good a way of drawing attention to yourself as any I know," said Chaucer. "No, there's something more to it. Either something you're not telling. Or something you don't know you know. I haven't made up my mind which yet."

Fortunately for Whitey's peace of mind, Chaucer was prevented from coming to any immediate decision by an interruption. A door opened and into the long dining-room came Hydrangea. She had disappeared as soon as they had reached the house; for medical care and rest, Chaucer had said and refused to answer any more questions about the girl's status or role.

Her hands were bandaged where she had burnt them in wielding the flaming stick and she had experienced some difficulty in knotting the belt of the loose bedrobe she wore. During the past twenty years at some stage in most countries fashion had permitted the ostentatious display of nearly every part of the human anatomy, male and female. For his part, Whitey still found the most provoking of garments were those which, as now, gave brief and unpremeditated glimpses of shapely breasts. At least, he guessed they were unpremeditated though it was hard to be sure of anything nowadays.

"Feeling better?" asked Chaucer. "Ready for something to eat?"

"I'll have a drink," she said.

Whitey had risen to his feet. Good manners were very much the in-thing in American society at the moment. Chaucer had not moved and now the girl sat down without a glance in Whitey's direction, leaving him feeling absurd and stranded. He collapsed heavily into his chair, feeling a pulse of anger beginning to beat somewhere in his head.

"You took your time in coming," said Hydrangea casually, grasping with some difficulty the glass Chaucer offered her.

"You cocked it up a damn sight quicker than I expected. Even though I warned you."

"I'm sorry. That shooting at the end, I wasn't taking much in . . ."

"Someone tried to put Mr. Singleton out of his misery. He got away."

"Yes. Still you got him."

They both examined Whitey with an emotional detachment which he found infuriating, and also rather frightening.

Chaucer shrugged.

"Yes," he said.

"Can we talk?" asked the girl.

Chaucer clapped his hands and a Striker came in immediately.

"Mr. Singleton," said Chaucer, "You must be tired after your exertions. Perhaps you'd like to retire."

There wasn't much choice. In fact, none. Whitey emptied his glass and rose, swaying slightly. He leaned forward resting his left hand on the table and wagging the index finger of the right at the girl.

"Next time," he said rather thickly, "next time you burn."

Then, nodding emphatically and still wagging his finger he backed away till the Striker took him gently by the arm and led him from the room.

He was awoken by the sound of his bedroom door opening. It was pitch black and felt like three or four in the morning, the unholy hour when even lovers are asleep and the only night-callers are those with a truncheon in their hands, and an unmarked truck in the street. The perfect time to start psychoyuss, thought Whitey, the sickness of too-early-waking and too-late-fearing rising in his throat.

He sensed someone standing at the bedside, tried to prepare his muscles for counter-attack, felt the bedclothes pulled slowly off him, managed to lift his head from the pillow, but could manage no more.

Then his visitor was in the bed with him, the clothes were pulled over them and Hydrangea's voice whispered, "I've come to thank you."

He began to shake with nervous relief and could only hope it felt like uncontrollable passion.

"My mother told me to find a nice polite girl," he said with an attempt at lightness which sounded an octave higher than usual.

"You'll have to do the grafting," she said.

"What?"

"My hands. I'm not very good with clothes and things." They managed very well.

Afterwards he wanted to switch on the light but she wouldn't let him, saying it might draw the attention of the guardian Strikers.

"Don't they ever sleep?" asked Whitey.

"This place is a fortress," she answered. "Constant patrols."

"But why did Chaucer come to somewhere so

isolated? He must be very vulnerable?"

"On the contrary. He knows that it's the commando raid he has to worry about, not the frontal attack. And nearly all those who fight against the Clubs are trained in urban guerrilla tactics. Outside here it's like a jungle. Thorn hedges, briar, gorse; swamps and ponds; trip-wires everywhere; flood-lights that come on at irregular intervals, and a pack of guard-dogs like the Wild Hunt. The Strikers know it like the back of their hands. But anybody else . . ."

"How do you know all this?" he asked.

"I watch. And I listen."

"I've noticed. Tell me, who are you?"

She laughed quietly in the dark.

"My name's Mavis Chesterman, if that helps. It's not much of a name, is it? What was it you called me just now. Hydrangea? That's nice. Let's stick to that. If it's good enough for that particular moment in a relationship, it'll do very fine."

"OK. Hydrangea it is. Why did you hi-jack my plane? What were you doing at Coventry? What's your connexion with Chaucer?"

She half rose in the bed, turned to him and rested on one elbow. Her breasts lay on his upper arm. He felt that despite the dark she was closely scrutinising his face.

"You won't like it," she said finally.

"I'm inured to shocks."

"OK. I'm a crook. In fact I'm an American crook."

151

"With your accent?" he interjected.

"My parents were English. Like you, they got out when the Four Clubs took absolute control. Or rather a bit earlier. My father saw the way things were going and we dropped everything and left. That was about ten years ago. I was eleven."

She paused as though to look back on that unimaginable state. The darkness, so recently full of terror and then of passion, was now gentle, warm and soporific. Whitey felt himself sliding into sleep, despite his eagerness to hear Hydrangea's story. He pushed himself upright against the headboard.

"Go on," he ordered.

"We didn't take much with us and we didn't make much in America. But there are ways a growing girl can make a living. Soon, though, I found you can make more by lifting the mugs' wallets than letting them lift your skirts. And pretty rapidly I started thinking of the big time."

"Like stealing planes?" he asked ironically.

"No," she replied seriously. "That was a mistake but a necessary one. You heard about the big L.A. bank job?"

"You mean where they dug the hundred foot tunnel? Yes, I read about it. Some job!"

"Thanks," she said, ironic now in her turn. "It's nice when honest citizens admire your work."

"What! You're not saying that was you?" He was openly incredulous.

"None other," she said proudly. "And it was

152

my plan. Perfect. It took a man to cock it up. Or rather a lot of men."

"But you got away with it!" said Whitey. "All that money!"

"And the rest of the stuff out of the safe-deposit boxes. You'd never believe what we found! It was pretty bulky, you understand. But I had a nice little plan. Oh yes. The building the tunnel started in was an empty warehouse. But next to it was a nice full one, one large item in which was a consignment of tinned goods for a firm in Tokyo. We dumped half a ton of tomatoes in the river and repacked the cases with our loot."

"Ingenious," said Whitey. "Except that you'd have to go to all the bother of stealing it again in Japan."

"No sweat," she said. "The Tokyo firm was an office and a dockside storeroom. Owned by me. So we split up after the job and headed for Tokyo by different routes. That's when things started going wrong. One of us didn't turn up. He let himself get picked up on a speeding charge and when they saw who he was, they started questioning him hot. Worse though, the loot didn't come through. I rang the L.A. firm. They were sorry, an urgent order was found to be incomplete and had been made up with our consignment, but more tinned tomatoes were being sent express. Where had the original consignment gone, I asked. England, they told me proudly! That's why it was so urgent. They were among the first to be taking advantage of the new thaw in trade relations."

"And the man they captured?" prompted Whitey.

"Oh he talked. They all do after a time. Third degree, psycho-yuss, truth-drugs, something works in the end. We expected it as soon as an L.A. contact rang to say he'd been taken. So we were right off to the airport, me still in my oriental gear. Our plan was to do a few short hops round the Pacific. You sit on a plane too long and there's somebody waiting for you at the other end. Unfortunately the only plane with vacant seats leaving within less than three hours was the Sudan flight. Who wants to fly to a war? Still, we took it, even knowing that they'd be waiting for us at the other end. Then came the brilliant idea. Kill two birds with one stone. Take over the plane and head for England which (a) did not have an extradition treaty with the U.S. of A. and (b) did have our loot, all done up to look like packs of canned tomatoes."

"So the hi-jack was spur-of-the-moment stuff?"

"You bet. I mean, with the precautions they take nowadays, who premeditates a hi-jack? We were fantastically lucky. Till we got here. Then we stopped being fantastically lucky. Our claim to be political refugees soon had them laughing all the way to the dungeons. I don't know what happened to the others, but you saw what they did to me. When I got out, I had to stick with

154

Chaucer, you understand that. He was on his feet and active. There was a chance there. You were lying on your face in your underclothes. I couldn't chance being captured again."

He felt her shiver convulsively at the thought and put his arm round her comfortingly.

"You were quite right," he reassured her. "Absolutely right."

"I know. Just as you'd have been right to keep your mouth shut and chuck me on that fire at Coventry."

"You can't be a crusading journalist all your life without something rubbing off," he said lightly. "But you haven't explained just what you were doing there."

She shrugged so that her breasts moved interestingly against his chest.

"Chaucer got me out of London. I don't know why, perhaps I gave him a bit of cover. But since getting here, he's put me to work for him. I've no idea what it's all about most of the time. A couple of days ago he sent me off to Coventry. I had to make contact with a certain Supporter, whisper a couple of magic words, receive a packet and take it back to Chaucer. Only, I picked the wrong reffer. The rest you saw. It was very nasty. I'm beginning to think I've paid Chaucer what I owed him. Still, I'm a naturally grateful girl."

"Yes, I've noticed," said Whitey, pushing himself down in the bed. Her hands were no good, but she made a few exploratory motions with her body. He smiled in the dark and kissed her gently on the cheek and after a while she lay still in his arms and he felt that she was asleep.

Sleep of all things seemed best to Whitey also at this moment. There had been a time when he prided himself on being a four-or-five-times-a-night man. But that had been another night. Perhaps even another man. And there was always the morning to look forward to.

He closed his eyes and dropped into oblivion.

When he awoke it was broad daylight and Hydrangea was gone.

So much for his pre-breakfast plans, he thought swinging his legs out of bed. He washed and dressed quickly and took a look out of his bedroom window. There was a superb view over wooded parkland to a distant fold of hills. Something of the old England remained, perhaps even something worth barricading yourself in for, he thought as he caught a glimpse of a Striker with an Alsatian patrolling the grounds.

But it wasn't patriotic sentiment that had caused Chaucer to build up this defence system, it was realistic fear. He must be a very important Management man to be able to command such protection. The Coventry Strikers had known who he was and it was this as much as his superior armament that had enabled him to yuss them. But it *had* been a yuss, not an unqualified act of co-operation. There was a tension between the Management and the University Supporters' Clubs which might eventually bring something about. The Disciplinary Committee's use of psycho-yuss was symptomatic. True, the crowd had got carried away in the end, but Chaucer's Strikers looked as if they would merely have toasted the truth out of the girl from the very start. An interest in confession and conversion rather than just information could only spring from a passionately believed-in philosophy of the Club. He had got a whiff of it from Sheldrake, the Athletic trainer. History had proved that philosophy was usually the death of revolution. Once people stopped acting intuitively and sat down to rationalize their actions, disagreement was inevitable; and, persuasion having proved futile, the only way of resolving debate was violence. In private life in the old days, the courts had gone some way towards condoning the crime of passion. In public life, it was the crime of reason which met with general approval.

He turned from the window, unable to see where it was his thoughts were taking him. It was difficult to decide which path was best for his country. The way of the Clubs? or the way of King and his terrorists? or was there a third path which he himself might help people to find? Surely it was just a question of finding a way to harness the fanatical loyalty to the Club he met with everywhere.

Even Hydrangea, he thought tangentially, had displayed an amazing amount of loyalty in standing up to the psycho-yuss for over ten hours when she had nothing to lose by telling them whatever they wanted to hear. And her loyalty had been rewarded. Chaucer himself had come looking for her.

He took the thought down to breakfast with him.

"You've got two minutes," said Chaucer as he entered the dining room.

"Two minutes for what?" Whitey replied evenly.

"For breakfast. You're coming with me to Birmingham."

Hydrangea was nowhere in sight, though a used coffee cup indicated she might already have eaten. Whitey would have liked to help himself to the full range of dishes which had been prepared, but Chaucer proved to be a very precise man.

"Let's go," he said after what Whitey suspected was exactly one hundred and twenty seconds.

Outside, a small rather old and anonymous car was waiting for them. Chaucer motioned Whitey into the passenger seat and himself climbed behind the wheel.

"Fasten your seat belt," he ordered.

Whitey obeyed, asking, "Is this your public image car?"

"No. It's my private safety car. It doesn't offer itself as a target."

"I see. And just the two of us? Aren't you a bit worried about me?"

Chaucer laughed, a little hurtfully.

"Not much. Why should you want to escape?

Your underground friends tried to kill you to stop you talking. You'd have a hard time persuading the wankers you hadn't talked. In any case, you're not going anywhere without my agreement."

Whitey was puzzled by this until he thought to try to release his seat belt. It was locked fast across his chest.

"You *can* release this eventually, I hope?" he murmured.

"Eventually," said Chaucer. "You'll just have to hope we don't have a crash."

"I'll think about that one," said Whitey and settled back to enjoy the ride.

Nixon Lectures : Fifth Series

Documentary Material

2 (f) Extract from HANSARD report of Question Time in the House of Commons January 23rd 1986.

Mr. Butt: Does the Secretary of State for Home Affairs approve of the tendency of our regional centres to take on an individual identity sometimes at odds with our national identity?

Mr. Corbridge: If I rightly understand the question, my answer must be that I see no reason why Yorkshire, say, should not remain Yorkshire, rather than try to emulate Norfolk. (laughter.)

Mr. Butt: Is the Secretary of State perhaps unaware that in the matter of film censorship, say, films shown quite freely in London are not permitted to be written about, let alone seen in certain parts of the country?

Mr. Corbridge: I was aware of this and I greatly regret any inconvenience caused to the hon. Member. If he cares to mention the film he has missed, I am sure we can arrange a private viewing. (Prolonged laughter.)

Mr. Butt: That's about your level, man. Bloody frivolity.

Mr. Speaker: The hon. Member is out of order.

Mr. Butt: I apologise. Let me put my question another way. Is the Secretary of State happy that he could swear in Swinton but would be heavily fined for it in Sunderland, that he could send his children to nothing but 'free' schools in Derby and nothing but nineteenth century classics-and-games establishments in Bournemouth, that his wife could be arrested for the shortness of her skirts in Carlisle but could go around with her tits hanging out in Peterborough . . .

Hon. Members: Withdraw! Withdraw!

Chapter 11

The journey to Birmingham was uneventful. A little knot of Supporters attempted to flag them down at one point, but Chaucer had merely pointed the car at them and accelerated. No one was actually hit, but he left them scattered over the road by their efforts of evasion.

"You don't give autographs then," observed Whitey.

"No. Just make my mark."

"Tell me," said Whitey, "what are you in this for?"

"What do you mean?"

"Well, it's a dangerous business, isn't it? You've had plenty of chance to salt a few dollars away. Why don't you take off and enjoy your old age in the sun?"

"Reff me!" exclaimed Chaucer. "You really do think like your articles, don't you? Despite everything you've seen, everything I've said, you still think I'm some kind of gangster."

"Look at the facts," said Whitey. "The American midcentury gangsters ruled by terror; they demanded unquestioning loyalty to the gang, punishing any breaches of faith by death; they carved up their country into separate territories, each distrustful of the others and in a state of constant alert and occasionally open warfare; by one means or another they gained influence over the forces of law, the judiciary, the arms of government itself. Spot the similarities?"

"You're thinking in journalese," said Chaucer, unimpressed. "You could just as well have been giving me a history of European civilization."

"I was scared you'd say that," said Whitey gloomily. "The worst gangsters of all are those who forget about money and start thinking about history."

Suddenly Chaucer laughed.

"Tell you what," he said. "I think you just want to be shown we think you're important enough to try and convince you. An earnest of survival!"

Whitey looked at him with cool indifference.

"That's one way out of an argument," he said. But inwardly he felt greatly discomfited at the truth in his companion's comment.

"Where are we going?" he asked now, determined not to relapse into a silence which might reveal his concern.

"To work," said Chaucer. "Deep down inside me, I'm just a commuter."

Birmingham didn't seem to have changed much since Whitey's last visit some six or seven years earlier. The days of urban development were long past and the only visible signs of change in most of England's cities was the steady encroachment of shabbiness. Slum-Clearance had allegedly reached its triumphant peak in the early eighties, but neglect, disruption of services, and years of social uncertainty had resulted in an even more intensive period of slum-creation, reaching almost to a nineteenth century level.

Their destination turned out to be the one which Whitey had anticipated, Wanderers Heights, the monolithic skyscraper headquarters of the Club. Four Strikers appeared with guns ready as they drove into the brightly lit basement car-park, but they stiffened to attention as they recognized the car. Chaucer parked it neatly in a slot marked 'Manager'.

"Ambitious," commented Whitey.

"No. Just promoted," replied Chaucer. "A policy disagreement left the vacancy. I'm on my way to accept the post formally now."

Which explains the rush, thought Whitey, amused by Chaucer's obvious delight.

But who is it who actually *offers* such a post?

A Striker joined them in the lift which rocketed them up to the top floor, and he followed them into a small windowless room, furnished with a single armchair.

"You wait here," said Chaucer.

"For how long?"

Chaucer shrugged.

"Depends how it goes. May be for ever." He smiled as he spoke but Whitey was not amused.

"You won't be lonely," continued Chaucer, glancing at the Striker who had taken up an alert position by the door. "Compose an article. Or think of — what do you call her? — Hydrangea."

164

He turned and went out. Whitey heard the door being locked from the outside.

So, he thought, he knows about Hydrangea's visit last night. A plant — or just good internal security? And did it matter?

"Sit," commanded the Striker.

He sank into the armchair which was surprisingly soft and luxuriously upholstered. They treated their prisoners well here. Or perhaps, he decided more realistically, perhaps it wasn't just his comfort they were thinking of. To launch a sudden attack from the depths of this chair was almost impossible.

He began pushing himself upright to see what would happen.

"Take a look at the back of the chair, mister," said the Striker mildly.

He twisted round and examined the floral-patterned upholstery. A neat repair job had been done but the dozen or so bullet-holes were still visible to the careful eye. Whitey nodded an acknowledgement at the Striker, sank back in the chair and remained quite still till he heard a double knock at the door. The Striker replied and only then was the door unlocked. Two more Strikers stood there, guns at the ready. They're not very trusting, thought Whitey, rising at a gesture from one of the guns.

They took him only a few yards down the corridor stopping before a shining stainless steel door marked BOARDROOM. One of the Strikers knocked. Another pause, almost certainly for some unseen scrutiny.

Then the door slid open and Whitey walked through into a small blank ante-chamber with yet another steel door before him. This slid open as the one behind him snapped shut and he found himself looking into a spacious, airy room in the centre of which was a long polished table around which sat perhaps a dozen men. One of them was Chaucer.

"Come in, Mr. Singleton," he said.

Whitey stepped inside and the second door slid shut behind him.

The colour dominant in the carpets, curtains and upholstery was, forecastably, Wanderers blue, but the designs and materials had been chosen with some taste. Around the walls hung a multitude of pictures and a brief glance told Whitey that these were photographs of some of the great Midland teams of the past. In faded sepia was the Villa 'Double' side of 1897, proud and unsmiling, their shirts laced tight at the neck. Curiously the moustaches sported by most of them had become popular again and appeared in almost the same proportion in the Championship team of 1979. Present also were the West Bromwich Division Two side which won promotion and the Cup in 1931 and the Birmingham side they beat, while half a dozen action pictures demonstrated the skills of the great Wolves side of the fifties. And in a trophy case among a host of lesser cups and bowls, stood the Football Association Cup itself which had been held by

Aston Villa at the time of the dissolution of the League.

"Gentlemen," said Chaucer. "May I introduce Mr. Whitey Singleton?"

"Blest, Singleton," said the man at the head of the table, large and solid still, though clearly in his sixties.

"Sorry," he added, glancing at his companions with a smile.

For what? wondered Whitey. Being polite to a prisoner?

Something about the big man was familiar though he couldn't quite place it.

"Take a seat," said the big man.

"Thanks," said Whitey, sitting in the chair which had been placed ready for him at the foot of the table. Almost immediately he jumped up again and went across to the wall where he stared hard at one of the old photographs.

"Billy Wildthorpe," he said suddenly. He turned round. The big man had joined him. "You're Billy Wildthorpe. I saw you play when I was a lad."

"Did you now?" said Wildthorpe delighted, clapping his hand on Whitey's shoulder. "Did I have a good game?"

"My dad," answered Whitey slowly, "used to say you played football like a gorilla with a pound of mustard up its arse. But yes, the day I saw you, you had a good game."

Wildthorpe had played for the one club all his life and when his playing days were over it had seemed natural that he should stay with them and eventually become manager. By the time of the dissolution, he had become a figure as respected and revered as Busby in the sixties. For a while as the Four Clubs began to emerge from the anarchy which followed the great police strike of 1985, the names of Wildthorpe and others highly placed in football's old hierarchy had received some prominence. But generally they had been figureheads only and when the politicians, the demagogues and the gangsters began to take over, one by one they had disappeared.

But not completely, it seemed. Whitey looked slowly round the table, checking his memory for other familiar faces. These men wore no flamboyant Supporters colours, but dark anonymous business suits, rather out of date in their cut. A Board of Directors twenty years earlier must have looked very like this.

Only one other face was at all familiar, a narrow, lined face, skin creased like grey flannel except for the shining smoothness of the completely bald head. But no name would come. Or rather at a very early stage of awareness, his mind rejected the only name that would come as making no sense, here and now.

Wildthorpe led him back to his seat and stood over as he sat down.

"Well, you know me, son. I won't introduce you round the table, but these gents you see here are all Club Directors. We've been talking about you this morning. You were high up on the agenda. Does that surprise you? Well, never mind. You've had an exciting time since you came back, I gather. And you've been keeping some bad company, running around with a smelly pack of anarchist wankers. But Mr. Chaucer assures us that your connection with them was more accidental than idealogical, is that right, Mr. Chaucer? Such reffing strange words for a plain man to have to use."

It was like plunging back into time, sitting in front of the television on a Saturday night watching recorded highlights of a couple of games and listening to this voice dissecting a game, a player, or even a commentator, the whiles claiming that the speaker was a plain, simple man, easily duped.

"Now, you've been writing a lot about this country and the Four Clubs in the past few years. Me, I'm not much of a reader, not since the sports pages went and that was just for laughs. So perhaps you could tell me in a few words, just so's I'd have it from your mouth with no fear of misrepresentation, exactly what you'd like to see happen in this country?"

Wildthorpe finished, stuck his left index finger in his ear in a gesture that hadn't changed in thirty years and screwed it around as he regarded Whitey expectantly.

Whitey tried to collect his thoughts, but a cold fear, worse than anything he had yet felt, was frosting his mind. He felt certain he knew now what was happening to him. These were the insidiously gentle and reasonable beginnings of high-level psycho-yuss. The path that lay ahead led out of this comfortable room to a public place, a hall or even a stadium, where eventually — after perhaps ten hours, perhaps a hundred and ten — he would see the error of his ways and make a public admission. If his resistance proved strong, he might at some point be shown the promise of pain, as Hydrangea had been shown the fire, as the prisoners of the Inquisition were shown the instruments. But the control would be stronger and the final result even more certain. The only possible source of help was King and the Jays and their only concern now seemed to be to get close enough to kill him.

"You may start, Mr. Singleton," said Wildthorpe mildly.

Reff it! thought Whitey yawning widely and convulsively. He might in the end cringe and qualify and contradict and recant, but while he was in control, before fatigue and fear had bent his mind, he would speak his mind.

"I'll spell it out simply enough for even a very plain man to understand," he said, looking straight at Wildthorpe. "If a society erects an ideal and works towards it, that's civilization. If a society takes the basic common denominators of human behaviour and uses these as its framework, that's barbarism. The Four Clubs system is barbaric. It represents the nadir of the long slide into chaos which began in 1914."

"Nadir," interrupted Wildthorpe. "That's the

lowest point, isn't it?"

Whitey nodded.

"But how can this be the lowest point, son? I mean, wouldn't we all be pulling your fingernails off and sticking electrodes into your balls if this were the lowest point?"

A threat, thought Whitey. An obvious threat. He felt unable to answer, but Wildthorpe hadn't finished in any case.

"No. Surely if there was a slide, and I don't dispute it, I've lived longer than you, son, and seen worse things, if there was a slide, surely the Clubs have halted it? Surely because of the Clubs things have levelled off? Far from being the nadir, the Clubs were the turning point, the saviours of society!"

He sat back triumphantly.

"No," said Whitey, finding his voice. "No. The establishment of the Clubs was something new, not just a point on the slide. Even a downhill movement still leaves you in relation to the heights. Rome in its decadence is still on a different plane of human existence from that inhabited by the barbarians. What the Clubs have done is publicly deny the ideal. They have accepted the common denominators of greed, lust, the rule of force, and by accepting, encouraged them. They have made evil their good, injustice their law, indulgence their morality. They are the antithesis of civilization!"

He paused. He had been shouting and the reverberations of his words drummed momentarily round the room.

"Well," said Wildthorpe, "I don't know about the others, but you've lost me. Was that the kind of thing you wrote in your articles? If it was, I'm very glad I didn't try to read them."

"In fact," said Chaucer smoothly, "if I'm not mistaken, Mr. Singleton was quoting directly from one of his recent pieces at the end."

"Quoting himself?" said Wildthorpe. "Well, that's novel. We used to have a Prime Minister who was for ever doing that. Lot of good it did him in the finish. Right, son. You've described what you think the disease is. What do you suggest as the cure?"

Whitey was discovering that there was a certain pleasure to be derived out of burning boats and bridges. If a man is going to be condemned, he himself might as well speak the words which will damn him.

"It's simple," he said. "First the dissolution of the Four Clubs and all that they stand for in terms of regional government and loyalties. Next, a return to central government and the rule of law. When this happens, the rest is detail. Like the re-establishment of our education system, the cleaning up of our towns both literally and meta-phorically. Oh, and I mustn't forget to mention, the trial and punishment of those criminal elements who have taken advantage of the chaos of the last decade for their personal gain."

He glared righteously down the double line of men seated before him, focussing on the expressionless face of Wildthorpe who had resumed his place at the other end of the table.

"That it?" the man now asked.

"That'll do for starters," said Whitey.

"You should have gone into Parliament," said Wildthorpe. "While you could, that is."

A small ripple of laughter washed round the table.

"Well, now we know where you stand," continued the big man. "So, let's get it straight, you see as the country's first and greatest need reunification. That is, the Clubs shedding their power and a return to some form of centralization?"

"Not some form. A specific form," interjected Whitey. "A Wanderers' conquest of the rest of the country would be no good."

"No, I see that. But if there were a treaty between the Clubs, a voluntary association, you'd be willing to support this as a first step?"

Where the hell is all this leading? wondered Whitey. He could still see nothing but the jeering crowds and the broken mind at the end of it, but the route was proving even more circuitous than he had imagined.

"Yes, I suppose so," he answered. "A small step, but the right direction."

"Good," said Wildthorpe leaning back and smiling expansively. "Then, with your agreement gentlemen, I think we may now invite Mr. Singleton into our confidence."

There was a pause. Then the bald head on

Wildthorpe's left inclined slightly and started a tremor of assent running round the table like a *feu de joie.*

"Right," said Wildthorpe. "We're not here to argue a case for the Four Clubs, Mr. Singleton, though I could easily do so, never doubt that. But it may be they've served their purpose. Their main disadvantage is an economic one. Great Britain, as was, is still a member of the Common Market, at least on paper. Mind you, they've been debating what to do about us for ten years now, but they've never got round to expelling us. But things are getting tight."

Whitey could well imagine it. He had travelled widely on the Continent in the past few years and knew that irritation with Britain's internal affairs and their effect on Europe as a whole was reaching unbearable proportions. There was a large Colony of former British political leaders now living a curious half-life in Brussels and they were constantly on the alert for chances to exacerbate matters. The expulsion of Britain from the European Community was a very real threat. Some extremists even muttered about annexation, but Whitey discounted this. Expulsion was the real danger. With all former Commonwealth ties now completely severed and transatlantic relations the worst ever, separation from Europe would mean death.

"Some of us, ones not without influence, reckon the time has come for the country to be reunified. In fact, in a sense," added Wildthorpe looking round the table with a grin, "it's never really been divided."

Hobhouse! thought Whitey. The block was down now and the name slipped through quite easily. The bald-headed man was Henry Hobhouse, whose career with London clubs had paralleled Wildthorpe's in the Midlands. Obviously the parallels had continued into the world of politics and Hobhouse now occupied a corresponding position in the Athletic hierarchy. No wonder Wildthorpe had apologized for saying 'Blest'!

The others too. No names came, though some younger faces were now emerging from the middle-aged blanks which confronted him. United and City must be here too, he had no doubt.

"So," he said, "the old Association still exists."

"Exactly!" said Wildthorpe. "It was always like this, even in the old days. The lads would knock hell out of each other on the park and the supporters would have a punch-up on the terraces, but that didn't stop you having a drink and a friendly chat with old mates in the director's room."

"The only thing is, Mr. Wildthorpe," observed Whitey grimly, "it stopped being a game a long time ago."

"It did. Longer than you think, son," answered Wildthorpe.

"In fact I sometimes wonder if it ever really was a game. Anyway, the point is, things are getting moving once more. And you've just happened to drop in at the right time. You might be able to do us, and incidentally yourself, a bit of good."

"What had you in mind?" asked Whitey.

"Simple. We need a voice that will be listened to. Not just diplomatically, anyone can make that kind of noise. But publicly, so that the people we're dealing with can feel their own voters breathing down their necks."

"You mean, you want a P.R. man?" asked Whitey mockingly.

"That's it. You think about it a moment."

"And the alternative?"

Wildthorpe spread his arms and shrugged in an uncharacteristically exotic gesture.

"What do you want me to do? Make threats so that you can refuse indignantly? Or perhaps so you can accept reluctantly? No. You just choose, Mr. Singleton. Take your time. We're due for some coffee now."

He nodded at Chaucer who rose, went to the door and spoke into a microphone. A few seconds later the door slid open and a girl, eye-catchingly dressed in a bright blue cat-suit, pushed in a wheeled trolley laden with coffee. Whitey noticed that many of the men at the table had turned away, probably to minimize the risk of recognition. Not that it was high, these were not well-known faces. But it wouldn't be diplomatic to let the ordinary Club supporter know that City, Athletic and United men were being entertained in Wanderers Heights.

176

"Thank you, love," said Wildthorpe. "We'll serve ourselves."

The girl nodded. She was really very attractive if perhaps just a trifle over-made-up. She was in the process of lifting a large coffee-pot. Suddenly there flashed in Whitey's mind a picture of Hydrangea walking down the aisle of the jet, carrying a coffee tray before her. This girl was very different from Hydrangea, taller, slimmer, brown-eyed. But the same sense of something wrong was prodding at his stomach.

Their eyes met. He was certain he'd seen her before. But where? And what did it matter?

She put the coffee-pot down and began to open the drawer on the trolley in which cutlery was kept.

In a shower. Even as the answer came to Whitey he was leaping forward. In a shower scrubbing purple dye off his body. Her hand came out of the drawer with a gun in it. The trolley was a barrier between them. He hurled himself at it as she fired, missing. The trolley caught her in the midriff and she doubled up firing twice more, wildly, desperately. Coffee cups showered to the floor, shattering against each other. Chaucer stepped forward now and chopped the girl twice beneath the ear with the edge of his hand. She fell backwards without a sound.

Whitey picked himself off the floor and examined himself for damage. Nothing, except a great weariness which seemed to start somewhere behind his eyes and spread inexorably through the whole of his body. Looking round, he saw that the girl's bullets had not been entirely in vain. The glass of the Cabinet holding the F.A. Cup had been shattered and the cup itself had a jagged hole pierced through it. And Hobhouse, the man from Athletic, was nursing a badly bleeding left fore-arm and looking greyer than ever.

Wildthorpe was on his feet, his face twisted in anger.

"Is this it, then, Singleton? Is she one of the representatives of your civilized ideals? Is this the kind of progress you want?"

He thinks she was after him, thought Whitey. He's got a right to be angry.

He met Chaucer's gaze. The Manager raised his eyebrows quizzically.

He knows, thought Whitey. And knowing that, he knows there's only one thing I can decide.

He returned to his seat and absurdly began to wonder how that nice, safe, conventional war in the Sudan was going.

Documentary Material
2 **(g)** Sir Benjamin Coster's diary (Goth and
      Vandell, New York; 1991) Entry for
      March 6, 1987.

To Downing Street this morning. P.M. looking
very weary, whether with affairs of state or screw-
ing that little Welsh thing in the Treasury is hard
to say.

"Benjie," he said, "it's nonleague. The reffers
are blowing time on me."

I remarked I was sorry to hear him succumbing
to these attacks on our language, but he ignored
me.

"They've got regional government, they control all their own wealth and industry, but they
want complete autonomy with it. The bloody law
changes between Luton and Leicester, did you
know that? I get no support here either. That
lump of lard in the Home Office couldn't piss
holes in a snowdrift. I only put him in the job
because they told me he'd get cancer and would
be dead in the year. For Christ's sake, Benjie.
You own half of Fleet Street. You've got your
finger on the nation's pulse. What shall I do?"

"Dissolve Parliament," I said. "Otherwise you
may find it dissolving around you."

Afterwards to the Club, reflecting how thin a
boundary there is between incompetence and idi-
ocy. At the Club a truly terrible state of affairs.

The servants had withdrawn their labour and locked themselves in the bar from which they emerged only to hurl glasses and drunken abuse at the Committee. The police had been notified hours earlier but had replied they did not think it an emergency which warranted breaking their strike!

Chapter 12

"Mr. Singleton. Come on in! We have been most concerned about you."

Sam Exsmith, the American Ambassador, had had forty years experience of arranging his rubbery features into expressions fit for any and every kind of diplomatic situation. When he said he was concerned, he really looked concerned. But Whitey thought he could detect a wariness in the eyes which surveyed him from behind the steel-rimmed spectacles.

His own feelings were mixed. He supposed he should have felt safer than he had done for many days, sitting here in what was technically American territory in the heart of London. But for a variety of reasons, he didn't and it was clear that for Exsmith too this was more than just a simple reunion with one of his citizens who had got into trouble.

"Things have been really buzzing since that plane took off from Heathrow without you. Of course, they told us you'd decided to stay of your own volition and they regretted that your present whereabouts were not known. Well, we've heard all that before and I've had some of my boys trying to track you down since the day you arrived. But you move fast. Yes, you've got to admit it, you certainly move fast!"

"Like a rabbit with a stoat at its tail," agreed Whitey.

"Yes. Well, once you got out of Athletic territory, that was more or less it, of course. Hell, technically I'm the Ambassador to Great Britain, but we know what that means."

A great deal, thought Whitey. Since the discovery in 1986 that the C.I.A. had over a period of ten years bugged every room in the EEC headquarters in Brussels, America's diplomatic and trade links with Europe had been pared down to the thinnest lines possible and it was the stated ambition of several European politicians that they should be cut altogether. So the Embassy in London, even though it was only an Embassy to the Athletic Club, was of prime importance, especially if the astute Exsmith suspected the existence of the Association.

"I could hardly believe it when we got your letter. Especially not that bit about wanting to resume your British citizenship. Hell, I mean, after what you went through!"

"It's true," said Whitey. "That's one of the things I wanted to talk to you about. Just one."

The ambassador got up, opened a wall-cabinet and took out a bottle of bourbon. He poured a couple of glasses, flicked the switch on his intercom and said, "No interruptions for thirty minutes please. Except the White House."

"Now you've spoiled it," grinned Whitey.

"Sorry. OK, now, the floor's yours. What's

been going on? This is completely off the record, of course."

Off your record perhaps, thought Whitey but very much on everybody else's. He had heard enough recently to make him suspect that every organization, official and subversive, in the country had this office bugged. Presumably Exsmith knew this too. Well, that was his business. Whitey was certainly not going to be tempted to diverge from his script. In any case, he now half believed in it.

"The circumstances of my arrival in England don't need to bother us," he began. "That I didn't come by choice is obvious enough. But I'm a free agent now, I want you to understand that. I've moved around a lot, talked to a lot of people in the past couple of weeks. And though much that I've been attacking for half a decade now is still present and still deplorable, I've become more and more convinced that the time is ripe for change."

"You mean, revolution?" asked Exsmith in his interested cocktail-party voice.

"Hell no! That could come. It's very close. And in the last resort, it might be the only way. But I think it can be avoided. I think a change that starts at the top and works its way down, though it might be slower and less certain, will be a lot less bloody and destructive."

"And such a change is possible?" asked Exsmith blandly. He had picked up a pencil and was doodling on his blotter.

"Don't play diplomats!" ejaculated Whitey. "You've been approached. You know what's in the wind."

"I'm afraid that I can't discuss confidential diplomatic exchanges, not even with such a distinguished journalist as yourself. *Especially* not with such a distinguished journalist."

"Well, I'll say it first, shall I? Just to show I'm not pumping you. The Four Clubs are proposing a merger. The re-establishment of a satisfactory economic relationship with Europe is the main aim, but there's more than just that. At least I think there will be. This could be the first step to bring back the rule of sense and humanity to this country. And you've been approached because we need aid now. We need goods, we need money. Our rehabilitation in the European scene is not going to take place overnight. Meanwhile we need the help of a disinterested benefactor. We can't go to Brussels, cap in hand."

"Of course, you can't. That wouldn't do at all. Not *Great* Britain. And how nice it would be to be able to play the threat of an increasing off-shore American interest at the European gambling table!"

Whitey finished his drink.

"The political in-fighting's your field," he said. "Me, I'm just a writer. The first couple of my articles have gone off to my publisher. They're syndicated throughout Europe, as you know. I just called here to let you know I was safe and to give you notice of my intentions. That's all."

"Just a courtesy visit, eh? Well, I appreciate that, Mr. Singleton. But surely your new masters expect a little more than courtesy from you?"

The tone was sarcastic but as he spoke, Exsmith turned his blotter round and pushed it towards Whitey. On it the American had written, *Are you in trouble? Say the word and I'll fix for you to be air-lifted out in a couple of hours.*

"I expect they hope you'll report the truth to *your* masters. That I'm alive and well and working for a united Britain. And if that helps to convince them it's worth joining in the game, well, that's all for the good."

As he answered Whitey was scribbling on the blotter. *No, I'm fine. I think they're on the level and I want to stay. Anything you can find out for me, I'd be grateful.*

"I see," said Exsmith. "That sounds fair enough. Another drink?"

"No thanks."

Ring 722-589-605-9 after ten P.M. read the blotter.

"Sure?"

"Just a little one, then."

As his glass was refilled, Whitey bent forward, concentrating on imprinting the number on his mind.

"How's that? Enough?" asked Exsmith, passing the drink. Whitey nodded and the Ambassador quietly removed the inscribed layer of blotting paper and fed it into the teeth of the destructor which stood by his desk.

"What happens about my citizenship?" asked Whitey.

Exsmith shrugged.

"It's just about as difficult to give it up as it is to get it in the first place. You're quite sure about this?"

"Quite sure," said Whitey emphatically, but as he spoke he was shaking his head.

He thought about this later as he returned to the flat in St. John's Wood which Hobhouse had procured for him. Wildthorpe had been very insistent that he should publicly resume his British nationality as evidence of his sincerity. Whitey reckoned it was merely a method of putting him indisputably under U.K. jurisdiction if he stepped out of line, but in a paradoxical kind of way he found it comforting that there should now be a concern for even the mere appearance of legality. Without small straws like this, the temptation to accept Exsmith's offer would have been almost irresistible.

When he reached his flat, he wished he hadn't resisted it. Hobhouse was there with a couple of Strikers.

"Preds," said Whitey, remembering in time which Club territory he was in. "Does everybody in town have a key?"

He was surprised at the reaction. One of the Strikers swung the butt of his gun in a short arc which ended against Whitey's rib-cage.

"Sit down," he said unnecessarily.

"That's time, lads," said Hobhouse. "Wait outside."

The Strikers left and Whitey gasped, "This is the new humanity, is it? Only one blow at a time."

"Listen," said Hobhouse. He pressed a switch on a tape-unit which lay on the floor beside him. *How's that? Enough?* It was Exsmith's voice. A pause. *What happens about my citizenship?* Whitey recognized his own voice with the shock such recognition always brings.

"Right. What went on?" asked Hobhouse. His left arm was still heavily bandaged from the wound caused by the Jay girl's stray bullet. The last news of her was that she had been shot attempting escape. What this was a euphemism for Whitey preferred not to think, though he wondered if the reason for wanting to kill him had been extracted from her first.

"You heard it," protested Whitey. "Just a chat like we arranged."

"We heard the words. But listen again." His finger stubbed down on the button. "There. After enough. Something went into the destructor. Don't tell me it was a reffing toffee paper."

"Is that all?" demanded Whitey. "If you'd given me a chance, I'd have filled you in on everything. He wrote a note, asked me if I was OK; did I want to be taken out? I answered yes; no. That was it."

"You're lying," said Hobhouse calmly.

"Why should I lie? I came back, didn't I?"

"I'd have been interested to see you trying to do anything else."

"For Godsake!" exploded Whitey, "either you trust me or . . ."

"What?"

"Or I suppose you get your boys back in and start knocking me around."

"Unnecessary," said Hobhouse, shaking his head. "Just so you know I know you're lying. You're Wildthorpe's idea, not mine. Remember that. You take off, I lose no face. But if I catch you at it, you'll lose face and more besides. Boys!"

The Strikers returned and one of them picked up the tape-recorder while the other looked enquiringly from Whitey to Hobhouse.

The bald man shook his head.

"Home," he said. "Singleton, you stay here. Someone'll be in touch. An old friend I believe."

He left like an old-time Chicago gangster, one Striker going ahead to check the route was clear, the other one pace behind very much on the alert.

Whitey locked the door behind them and went into the bedroom to study the effects of the Striker's blow in the mirror. A dark bruise was already spreading to join the other paler bruises and fading scars which were the mementoes of his homecoming. He looked ten years older, he thought gloomily, studying his reflection. And it wasn't just the moustache he had started growing for security purposes. The relationship between those features and the youthful face which topped his weekly column was now so remote as to be imperceptible to the non-initiate. Suddenly the attractions of Exsmith's offer to get him out filled his being with such a sensuous longing that he had to sit down on the edge of the bath till it passed.

He was far from certain why he had not embraced the chance with the fervour he would have shown shortly after his arrival in England. Nearly a fortnight had passed since the meeting in Wanderers Heights and during that time he had become convinced of the genuine desire of the Four Clubs to recentralize government and get the economy back on the move. But the pendulum-swing theory, the idea that to return to the best you had to accelerate the worst, was the nearest thing to a political philosophy that was offered to him and this he found totally unconvincing. Why not escape then? he asked himself once more. To break an agreement reached *via* the threat of physical yussing could hardly be regarded as immoral. Yet there was a glimmer of hope in this situation, a chance that the turning point would be reached. And if he could help at all, it was from here, from within, not from the hotel-rooms, airport lounges, lecture halls, which seemed to have been his home for the past five years.

That was the noble, altruistic reason, he told himself sourly as he returned to the lounge and began preparing a snack meal. The other reason, a bit lower down but supporting all the rest, was purely egotistic. He was here because he was a journalist, a man of influence, a writer whose words were units of power in the international game. By being here, by accepting even the kind of grudging, suspicious support that people like Hobhouse were offering him, he was giving the brown eye to King and all the others who had sneered at the alleged futility of his articles.

He sat down and started eating a slice of rubbery bread and a cube of solid-state cheese. Rations here were far from the gourmet delights of Chaucer's country house. He had returned there briefly after the meeting with the members of the Association Board of Directors. Hydrangea had slipped in to see him, but he had treated her rather coolly, remembering that details of their last meeting seemed to have gone straight back to Chaucer. Careless talk was unsafe and it didn't matter if Hydrangea were the bearer of it or some tiny electronic bug. Or rather it did matter a great deal, but pretending it didn't matter was the best way for survival.

After that he had been transferred back into Wanderers Heights where he had talked, listened and written for ten solid days. His first two articles had been cautious and tentative in their expressions of hope that things might be taking a turn for the better in Britain. He had written a covering letter to his editor authenticating them, and talked to him on the transatlantic line. But Wildthorpe had decided it needed more than this to convince the outside world that there was no pistol being held at Whitey's head. Hence the transfer to London and the visit to the Embassy.

Pushing aside his plate, he rose, went into the bedroom and stretched out on the bed, switching on the bedside radio as he did so. The Athletic territory early evening news was on and he listened to it with a journalist's admiration for media manipulation. Slowly, a drop at a time, the process of diluting Club news with national news and national news with international had begun. There had been a riot in Manchester. A fortnight ago this would have been reported, if at all, with relish as evidence of the parlous state of City affairs. Now the speed with which the City First Team Strikers had stemmed the disturbance was remarked on, albeit neutrally. Europe was mentioned, briefly. Things were booming. The news from Brussels was good. Nothing was said of the long debate on Britain's proposed expulsion from the E.E.C.

Then his own name was mentioned.

"It was announced today that former journalist and escaped convict, Whitey Singleton, has reapplied for club membership. Singleton, jailed six years ago for terrorist activities, escaped after only a few months and has been living in America ever since. Now in a remarkable turn-about he has announced that he recognizes his former errors and wishes to reaffirm his old allegiances. Management reaction is cautious but not unfavourable, though the question of the uncompleted prison sentence is one that must first be answered."

Whitey switched off. That did it, he thought. They weren't leaving him any way out. Only Exsmith could offer him that, should he wish to take it. Which, of course, he didn't.

He tried to recall the number he had memorized from Exsmith's blotter, couldn't bring it to mind for a moment, felt a terrible panic rising inside his head, then the numbers formed and he subsided, sweating slightly with relief. His adopted country had offered him a lifeline. He would be a fool to let it go.

The doorbell rang. He approached it cautiously. Under the protection of the Association though he might be, this was still London and you didn't open your door to unknown callers.

"Yes?" he called.

"Strikers, Mr. Singleton."

"Authority."

He heard something fall into the letter-trap. He unlocked it and examined the plastic card that lay there. Still cautious, he went to the telephone, dialled a number that Hobhouse had given him on his first arrival and checked the details on the card. Satisfied finally, he opened the door.

The Striker stepped in, smiling amiably.

"What is it?" asked Whitey.

"You're to come with me."

"Why? Where?"

"Management orders friend. Quick as you can, eh?"

This from a Striker was the zenith of courtesy.

He must have been told to be nice.

A car waited for them in the street, its engine running. It started moving the moment Whitey stepped inside, but this did not disturb him. No one stayed still any longer than they needed to in the city streets and if you wanted to leave your vehicle for no matter how short a time, you booked it into one of the fortified car-parks whose attendants carried pick-handles.

The drive was soon over. There were no speed-limits for strikers and the lightness of traffic permitted fast driving.

Their destination was a tall old house over-looking Parliament Hill Fields. One thing the British economic recession of the past fifteen years had done was to save most of London's open spaces, though shanty towns and caravan slums had begun to cover some of the less fashionable parks. But people round here had enough wealth to employ their own Striker force to keep the squatters out.

The door of the house opened without any signal needing to be given and they walked straight in.

"Up the stairs," said his guardian Striker. "First floor. Right. In there."

There was a big oak door. Whitey opened it and stepped inside, finding himself as at Wanderers Heights in a small antechamber. They took real care of themselves, these people, he thought as he rapped on the steel door which faced him.

"Yes?" A man's voice.

"Singleton."

"Come in, do."

The door slid open. He stepped inside. Standing with his back to him looking out of an open window at the darkening fields, was a man. He turned now.

"Nice to see you again, Whitey. Preds."

"Sheldrake," said Whitey. "Sheldrake. I thought you were dead."

"A miraculous escape," said Sheldrake, his tone solemn but a broad smile on his lips.

It was the smile that did it. He would have worked it out in the end, but the smile actively encouraged disbelief.

He saw again Sheldrake in Oxford; uninjured, allegedly because he knew nothing; unworried, allegedly because he expected to be transferred.

But he *had* known something, and had admitted it freely and openly. He had known they were in Jesus College. And with such knowledge no enemy of the Jays could have expected to be released alive.

And suddenly Whitey knew why King had been so eager to have him killed rather than captured.

And he knew also that his chances of coming through this evening alive were nonleague to the point of non-existence.

Nixon Lectures: Fifth Series

Documentary Material

2 (p) Extract from speech made by the French Foreign Minister to the European Parliament, March, 1992.

La Grande-Bretagne n'est plus un seul pays, mais cinq, peut-être six. Avec lequel de ces pays faut-il traiter?

Son parlement a été dissous et ses représentants n'ont plus le droit de participer à nos conseils. À quoi faut-il donc parler?

Nos routiers refusent de traverser la Manche parce que tant de leurs confrères ont été récemment attaqués et volés sur les routes dela Grande-Bretagne. Ceux d'entre nos ouvriers français qui n'ont pas encore quitté le sol britannique restent silencieux depuis si longtemps que leurs familles s'inquiètent prolondément à leur sujet.

Les redevances sur le plan financier ne sont plus versées par la Grande-Bretagne. Les accords commerciaux ne sont plus respectés par la Grande-Bretagne.

Dans quel sens peut-on continuer à considérer ce pays déchu comme membre de notre communauté?

Chapter 13

"Once you got to London again, you were bound to bump into me, or hear me mentioned. And once you did that, well, I mean, it wouldn't have taken you long to begin to worry and wonder about my miraculous escape, would it? Perhaps I'm wrong. Distrust breeds distrust, however, and I'm too important to be put at risk. You do understand? So I arranged for us to talk."

"And the other fellow, Burdern? What about him?"

"Oh he was for real," answered Sheldrake negligently. "He was well protected so they needed me to set it up. Naturally they had to take me with them for appearances' sake and they chucked me in with Burdern, just to check that he'd told them all he knew. It was just as well they did! When he told me he'd got a 'bug' stitched into his gut, that really put us into extra time!"

"And the shooting."

Sheldrake shrugged.

"No point in dragging Burdern around. I was a bit concerned when I heard you'd got loose. That King! Yesterday's nappy-crapper and he thinks he knows it all."

"He did try to shoot me at Coventry. And arranged another try later," said Whitey, feeling absurdly defensive about King.

"So? You're here, aren't you? And a danger still. So tell me, Singleton, just whose side are you on? In theory you should be with us, the Underground I mean. In practice you seem to be levelling with Hobhouse and Wildthorpe and that lot. So where do you really stand?"

Whitey raised a wan smile.

"You can't really expect rational debate, can you? At the moment where I really stand is here, wondering what the hell I can say to stop you shooting me. You know it; I know it. It's hardly the atmosphere for truth and sincerity, is it?"

In a nearby room a 'phone sounded. Sheldrake looked as if he had been expecting it and quickly moved across to the door. The friendly Striker came in as he left.

"I seem to spend half my life in rooms with members of the First Team," observed Whitey. "We'll be getting a bad name."

"What?" said the Striker.

"I mean, they'll be saying that you're a lot of glibs," laughed Whitey.

"None of that," ordered the Striker, looking much less friendly now.

"Why? What's the matter? There's lot of it in Management, you know. Take a look at this."

He pulled open the door of a wall-cupboard selected at random. It contained what looked like a rather expensive set of crystal goblets and a decanter. Whitey picked it up and held it in the air to catch the light.

"What?" asked the Striker coming forward, full of prurient curiosity. "It's only a decanter."

"Have a look inside," said Whitey knowingly. The Striker peered into the cupboard and Whitey crashed the decanter down on to the exposed neck. Fortunately it did not break or the man's neck and Whitey's hand's might have been badly lacerated, but the Striker fell forward among the wine-glasses then slid back out, pulling the shelf with him. The noise this made was tremendous and Whitey was spared the agonies of rational choice as fear-provoked instinct took over and the black square of the open window suddenly let in a gentle breeze which rustled the curtains as though in invitation.

The invitation seemed less pressing when he clambered on the sill. These were tall houses and the shadowy vagueness of the garden below made the drop seem immense. Behind him a door opened. Whether it was Sheldrake or another Striker he didn't bother to find out. There was a shout. He jumped.

The ground hit him a lot earlier than he had expected. What he'd had in mind was something more like the descent of Lucifer, twisting and turning slowly in the air for nine days and nights. But there seemed no gap at all between the sill and the low though fortunately sturdy shrubs which contributed slightly to deceleration. His unpreparedness prevented tension and he rolled forward three or four yards, limbs flailing loosely, before fetching up against a slender tree. Laburnum, he thought for some reason as he pulled himself upright against its trunk and waited for his much overused nervous system to tell him if anything was broken. The lights that flashed on in his mind were just the familiar pinks and oranges of bruising and laceration, almost a disappointment in a way as it meant he had to keep on running.

The garden was not very deep and ended in a high smooth-faced wall. He leapt for the top, just reached it with the ends of his fingers, discovered it was lined with broken glass, and collapsed to the ground swearing and waving his hands in the air to assuage the pain.

At the open window someone was shouting angry instructions. No pursuers seemed to have come out of the house yet, but from the other side of the wall he heard running feet and, worst of all, the excited bark of a dog. It sounded like a large dog.

He stood upright once more, wondering if it was worth trying to get back into the house. Close-by he heard the rattle of a key in a lock. Whoever was outside had the wherewithal to get inside. If he could only locate the door in the wall . . .

It swung open almost into his face, admitting precipitously a combination of shapes which seemed to comprise a Striker and a huge Alsatian, with the dog very much in control. Its main object at the moment seemed to be to out-roar the angry man at the upper-window. Gratefully

Whitey slid round the door and stepped through the wall. The Striker had left the key in the lock. He pulled the door shut, turned the key, withdrew it, hurled it into the darkness of Parliament Hill, and followed it.

This was his mistake, he realized half an hour later. If you are being pursued in the open countryside, you don't try to escape by way of a small hamlet of a dozen houses. Conversely in the midst of any large urban area, the relatively small patch of open land is a trap. In every direction he could see moving flashlights and hear the throaty calls of hunting dogs. He had waded through two ponds in his effort to break the trail and had at least succeeded in confusing the beasts. But it was a delaying tactic only, he thought as he crouched wet and shivering behind on oak tree. The great branches vaulting outwards not far above his head seemed to offer a promise of security, but to climb up among them would be fatal, he was sure. His flight had given Sheldrake the opportunity he must have planned to invent of killing him, and once the dogs had him treed, it would be like shooting rooks for the Strikers.

His only real hope was to break through the line of hunters and get back into the streets and buildings. And then . . . a choice. Ring the number Exsmith had given him and ask to be taken out. Or contact Hobhouse and tell him that Sheldrake was a Jesuit. A difficult decision, but one which he was presently a long way from having to face. Strangely enough the only person he felt he would like to be able to contact now for help and advice was the ingenious King. Who would kill him, of course, but that apart, he'd know how to slip out of this trap.

He looked up into the tree once more. It really was tempting. That was the difference, of course. King would not have been tempted. But he might have been inspired.

Carefully Whitey began to climb the oak.

Five minutes later he was crouching in the shallows beneath the bank of the last pond he had walked through. He was colder than ever now, having removed his jacket and left it spread out over a couple of branches as high up the oak as he'd been able to penetrate. Then he had dropped to the ground and as nearly as possible retraced his tracks to the pond, re-entering it and wading round to the far side. His hope, based on memories of some childhood story, was that the dogs, casting round the pond for his scent, would pick up and follow his double track to the tree. Once there, if the Strikers believed they had him trapped, and if they summoned all the searchers to be in at the kill, and if they . . . he pulled himself up. One 'if' at a time was all he could hope for.

And even that seemed a vain hope a few minutes later.

A bunch of Strikers and a dog arrived at the pond, following the track of his first entry into the water. As anticipated, they began following the line of the bank to pick up his exit spoor. But instead of moving round the pond clockwise which would have brought them shortly to the oak-tree trail, they set off in the other direction which meant they would pass his hiding-place first.

'Hiding-place' was too fine a term for it. He was crouched low beneath a bank only a couple of feet high, his only protection to the landward side being a few ferns which drooped over the surface. He was better protected to the water-ward side by a water-logged branch in which were tangled various other pieces of flotsam. The water stank and was full of bits of junk and debris. The thought of sinking any lower in it was nauseating but as the lights and the dog approached nearer and nearer, he could delay no longer and slowly he slid down beneath the branch till the water lapped at his chin.

His self-abnegation was rewarded. The searchers passed by without pause and moments later, the dog barked, there was an encouraging murmur from its handler and the party broke away from the pond and headed towards the rise on which the oak grove stood. He raised his head above the level of the bank and watched them go, shapes at first and then only a moving tangle of lights.

After a while the lights stopped, untangled themselves and formed a loose pattern. There was a brief silence. They had reached the tree, must be standing around it. He envisaged the dogs standing against the broad trunk, forelegs out-splayed, trying to track the scent into the leafy darkness above.

Then, a shout. A wild chorus of barking. A blowing of whistles. Other lights began to converge on the oak grove. They must have spotted the foreign darkness of his jacket in the topmost branches. For a few moments they thought they had him. But no more than a few moments.

With difficulty he pulled himself out of the stinking ooze which lined the pond and pointing himself at the nearest line of silhouetted houses, set off at a laboured trot. Behind him he heard a shot and thought for a second he had been spotted. It was followed by a lengthy fusillade and he realized the Strikers were filling the bush of the oak-tree with lead. When they stopped and no bullet-torn body crashed to the ground, they would realize their mistake. But it would be too late, he told himself optimistically. Another twenty yards and he'd be out of the open. The shooting stopped. Now they'd probably send someone up the tree. He'd find the jacket. They'd start the search again. But he'd be long gone. Down back alleys, along protective canyons of tall buildings; perhaps he could break in somewhere, steal a car, find a 'phone. The options were endless.

The options ended.

As his feet struck tarmac, a light sprang out of the darkness and stung his unprepared eyes.

"Just stop there," came a command. Behind

the lights he could dimly make out two Strikers. Both had guns pointed unwaveringly in his direction. He stood still, slack with defeat.

"Shall we finish it now?" asked one of his captors.

"Blow up the others first. Silly reffers, they almost let him out. Let's rub their noses in it."

The notion seemed to amuse. Three long blasts on a whistle followed. They woke Whitey to the desperateness of his situation.

"Listen," he said urgently. "Ring Hobhouse. Tell him I'm here. Don't do anything till you've talked with Hobhouse."

"Who's Hobhouse?" asked one of the Strikers with what seemed genuine puzzlement. They really don't know, thought Whitey. Why should they? Too young to remember him as a manager, and probably only his personal team knew him as a Director. "Perhaps it's his solicitor," said the other and they both roared with laughter.

The first of the main band of Strikers was approaching now, a long way ahead of the disappointed mob who had been gathered round the tree. Perhaps extra blood-lust had given him strength to hurry to the kill thought Whitey as the figure came rushing through the darkness.

"What kept you so long," called one of the two captors derisively.

There was no answer, just heavy, out-of-breath panting. And there was something odd about the newcomer's running style, thought Whitey. It brought something to mind. Something very ordinary. A woman running for a bus.

It struck his captors too. A second torch was flicked towards the new arrival. Red First-Team track-suit. Regulation machine-pistol. But the face . . .

"It's a reffing woman!" exclaimed one of the Strikers.

It was the last thing he said. The reffing woman was firing now. She must have been dazzled by the torchlight, but it provided her with an unmistakeable target. The torches shattered and the men behind them folded up beneath the murderous hail which continued till the magazine was empty.

"Hello," said Whitey.

"Are you going to stand there all night? You'll catch your death of cold," said Hydrangea.

The pride a man feels in being independent, resourceful, his own master, is matched only by the pleasure of abdicating to someone else complete responsibility for his health and well-being. Once having done this, Whitey was able almost to enjoy the quarter-mile run with the Strikers close behind, followed by the ten minute drive at a speed potentially suicidal even if the driver had been using lights. The driver he recognized without surprise as the bulky, pale-faced man who had been involved in the plane hi-jack ten thousand years ago.

The car finally came to a brief halt in a street which Whitey felt vaguely must be in

Kensington, though he would not have been unduly troubled to find that his sense of direction had misled him and he was in Biggleswade. Hydrangea pulled him out on to the pavement and the car continued its progress rather more steadily.

"Let's get inside," said Hydrangea, making for the main entrance of the block of flats outside which they were standing. It was a good idea, thought Whitey. You didn't hang around the streets of London after dark, if you were wise. Already a couple of shadowy figures had detached themselves from the night at the end of the street and were moving slowly in their direction.

Hydrangea took him to an apartment on the second floor. The rooms were spacious and the decoration looked as if at one time it had been luxurious. But it had been long neglected and the present furnishings were sparse and functional. But to Whitey it had the holy atmosphere of sanctuary that a church must have had to a medieval fugitive.

"If I were you," said Hydrangea, "I'd get out of those clothes. Bathroom's through there. The water should be hot and you'll find a robe you can use till your pants get dried. I'll do some coffee."

"Great," said Whitey sincerely.

"Great," he repeated with undiminished sincerity twenty minutes later as he sank into one of the tatty and peeling old leather armchairs and sipped the scalding coffee which awaited him.

"You make things rough for yourself," said Hydrangea. She had changed out of the First Team gear and was wearing the kind of soft frilly feminine dress only glibs ever wore in public.

"Yes," answered Whitey, looking at her approvingly. "Lucky you came along."

"Very lucky," she agreed. "But not entirely so. I like a bit of credit. When they all congregated round that tree, I thought you'd had it. Only I couldn't believe you were stupid enough to get yourself trapped up a tree. And if you *were* up the tree, you certainly weren't stupid enough to pretend that you weren't when thirty Strikers are all standing around below dying to let their guns off. No, you'd have dropped down and started talking. It would have done you no good, but that's what you'd have done. So I started backtracking you. I've read my Fenimore Cooper too. That's how I had such a good start on the rest when those two poor wankers blew the whistle on you. Not entirely luck."

"No," agreed Whitey, sipping his coffee. "Well, so that's how it happened, is it? Good. Though of course it doesn't quite altogether explain what you were doing wandering around disguised as a Striker in the first place."

"Looking for you, of course."

"Yes. I see that. But how did you know where to look for me?"

"We have our methods," she said enigmatically. Somewhere in the flat a 'phone rang, then stopped as though someone had picked it up, Hydrangea cocked her head attentively.

"And who is 'we'?" asked Whitey.

"Just a few friends."

"Are you still working for Chaucer?"

"No. Not exactly. Excuse me."

She rose and left the room, whether to evade his question or to consult with the person who'd answered the 'phone, Whitey was not sure. He gave her twenty seconds before following. The old leather armchair was surprisingly comfortable and he could easily have slipped into sleep just sitting there. But there were things he had to know.

He turned the door-handle as quietly as possible and looked through the crack into an empty bedroom. Another door led out of this. It was slightly ajar and though he could not see through it, he could hear voices.

He moved quickly across the bedroom. The floorboards creaked warningly and he hoped that the conversation in the next room would be loud enough to cover this.

"How the hell should I know?" a man's voice was saying. "He said he'll get over as soon as he can."

"You're not exactly putting your best foot forward to impress me," said another male voice, mockingly. Whitey recognized it instantly. "Why, for instance," it continued, "don't you invite Mr. Singleton in, instead of letting him stand in a draught by the door?"

The door was immediately thrown fully open. Hydrangea looked at him accusingly. A bearded man with a gun in his hand faced him menacingly. And from a tall, wheel-backed chair to which his left hand was manacled by a pair of handcuffs, King smiled at him welcomingly.

"You'd better tell me all about," said Whitey ignoring the bearded man's gun and stepping into the room. "Hello King."

"Hello, Whitey."

The room was furnished as a small study. It contained a couple of chairs, a filing cabinet, a bookcase and a desk. On the desk were a lamp, a typewriter, and a telephone.

Whitey looked down at the 'phone. The number was printed on the base. 722-589-605-9.

"So the Embassy employs bank-robbers now, does it?" he said to Hydrangea. "And keeps pet terrorists chained up next door to the bedroom? You really had better tell me all about it."

He felt so in command of the situation that his principal reaction when the bearded man hit him over the head with his pistol-butt was surprise. He was still feeling surprised when he woke up half an hour later and found Exsmith peering down at him with a face full of concern.

Nixon Lectures : Fifth Series

Audio-Visual Material

1 (f) Animated cartoon shown on children's tv comedy show.

SYNOPSIS

An Athletic Supporter, a City Supporter, a United Supporter and a Wanderers Supporter are arguing about which of them is the best shot.

The Wanderers Supporter throws a bottle into the air and shoots it before it can reach the ground.

The City Supporter throws two bottles and shoots them both.

The United Supporter throws three bottles and shoots them all.

The Athletic Supporter throws four bottles. We hear shots but none of the bottles breaks.

"I must be the worst shot of them all," he says despondently into the camera which then moves back to show the other three Supporters lying dead behind him.

Lecturer's Note: A version of this cartoon was shown on all Club networks, with the roles changed appropriately.

Chapter 14

"Let me explain, Mr. Singleton," said Exsmith. "It sounds complicated, I know. In fact it *is* complicated, unnecessarily so, I believe. But back home complexity impresses, as you know.

"Anyway, two things. For some time we've had some points of contact with the Underground movement here, nothing concrete, you understand. We don't supply arms or funds or anything of that nature. Oh no. On the other hand while there's a possibility that this movement might one day provide the legal government of a re-united Britain, then it's my job to keep the door open."

"Ouch!" said Whitey as Hydrangea pressed the cold compress over-solicitously to the lump on his head. Exsmith seemed to take the noise as encouragement.

"However, we like to have our own people near the centre of things. The Underground, quite naturally, is not willing to share all its secrets with us."

He beamed avuncularly at King who smiled sneeringly in return.

"Infiltration at low level is easy enough, of course. But it's more difficult to get to the top. So someone at home hit upon this plan of getting the Four Clubs, or some of them at least, to actually hire our agents."

"You mean the Los Angeles bank robbery and the hi-jack were just part of a cover story?" asked Whitey.

"I'm afraid so. It is over-complex, isn't it? And the money actually turned up in the tomato cases. Faked, marked notes, of course. It's fascinating to watch their progress throughout Europe. You'd be amazed at what's going on.

"So, the idea is, our agents ask for political asylum, which is very suspicious. Then it turns out they're bank robbers on the run, which immediately makes them credible and acceptable. Chaucer, the United Assistant Manager, is in prison here. We asked our friends in the Underground if they could arrange for this lady whom you know as Hydrangea, I believe, to be put in the same cell as him. The idea is that they might strike up some kind of acquaintance. Unfortunately it was not possible to foresee the kind of treatment she would be submitted to in the Scrubs."

"I should have thought it was pretty obvious," said Whitey sharply.

"Perhaps so. Well, it can't have been pleasant, not even in the course of duty."

Whitey glanced at Exsmith keenly but he seemed to be deadly serious.

"And Chaucer's own reaction. Well, that was certainly not to be expected from a man in high public office. Then you were chucked in with them, an additional complication. But as it turned out, a fortunate one."

The Ambassador nodded approvingly.

"It meant that when the escape plan was put into operation that night, you were able to assist Hydrangea to get out. And you gave her a second chance to get attached to the man, Chaucer."

"So that's why you abandoned me." Whitey looked sadly at the girl.

"What else could I do?" she asked. "When I got to Birmingham with him and he was able to check out my story, he offered me a deal. I work for him and he'd try to get his hands on those packs of tomatoes with the loot in them. I must have looked good to him, an experienced criminal with none of these disturbing club loyalties to interfere with my freedom of action. Naturally I took the deal. Things were going well till I got taken on the Coventry campus."

"Some of your friends arranged that, I believe, Mr. King," said Exsmith.

"What!" exclaimed Hydrangea. "But I was acting as a go-between."

"A go-between what?" demanded Whitey.

"The Association and the Underground, of course. The Directors had set up a link. They hoped the Underground might be willing to help in the plans to reunite the country. After all, that's one of the things they've been protesting about."

Whitey groaned.

"How could anybody be so naive!"

Exsmith shook his head disapprovingly. "Get this straight Mr. Singleton. No-one's being naive in this business. Devious, dishonest and deceitful, yes. But not naive."

"OK," said Whitey. "King. Why did your people drop Hydrangea in it?"

"Simple," said the young man cheerfully. "We weren't interested in any such deal with the Clubs. But we thought it would be nice to stir things up for Chaucer. The idea was, the girl here would soon be taken apart by the Disciplinary Committee and reveal all. Imagine the uproar there would have been! But unfortunately she held out, you did your perfect gentle knight bit, and Chaucer turned up to protect his interests."

Whitey looked round the assembled faces. They seemed to be united in expressing approval of this subtle tactic, even Hydrangea's. She caught the expression on his face and ran her fingers gently through his hair.

"Don't look so disapproving," she chided him. "I got out, didn't I? Thanks to you. Such things happen."

"Yes, and if it wasn't that you'd helped her then and she got a rush of gratitude to the head, you would not be here tonight, Mr. Singleton," said Exsmith gravely. "Hydrangea's back in London accompanying Chaucer who's helping set up the Wembley conference."

"The what?"

"They don't tell you much, do they?" said

Exsmith. "Don't worry. No doubt they'll get round to it. They'll want it splashed in one of your forthcoming articles.

"Anyway, Chaucer had set up another meeting with the Underground. He's an optimist that man. He thinks the Coventry business was just a mischance. So Hydrangea gets the go-between job again. At the same time, we, that is the Embassy, are wanting to strengthen our contacts for reasons which will become manifest. So we kill two birds with one stone. Hydrangea gets Chaucer's Strikers' protection to meet with Mr. King here to discuss *our* business. How do you like that?"

"Not much," said Whitey. "You mean, Chaucer knows about this place?"

"No. Of course not. They meet in a car, go off for a ride. Your name's mentioned. Mr. King indicates that tonight you're going to be relegated, as I think the term is. You've joined the opposition."

"He was trying to relegate me before I did that," said Whitey looking at the amused King.

"So he was. To stop you exposing one of their top inside men. Mr. Sheldrake, I presume."

King stopped smiling. Exsmith shrugged self-deprecatingly.

"An elementary deduction, given all the facts. Hydrangea brings Mr. King here, puts him under guard, rather to his surprise, I guess. And off she goes to try to pull you out of the fire."

"Thanks," said Whitey to the girl, realizing

now the full extent of his debt to her. Despite Exsmith's chatty manner and King's affability, neither of them was going to forget this piece of independent action in a hurry.

"But I still don't see what you two have got in common," he went on. "I should have thought that the Association's plans for dissolving the Four Clubs peacefully and realigning the country with Europe would have been very much in line with Washington thinking. While the kind of revolutionary left-wing workers' paradise the Underground want would have sent them screaming for their flintlocks."

"It's moral issues, not political systems we're concerned with here," said Exsmith sternly. "What my government and Mr. King share in common is a strong moral disapproval of the way the Four Clubs conduct their affairs. As you've written on any number of occasions, it's bloody, unjust and debasing."

"So the Association offers the chance of a change."

"On the contrary. You have been deceived, Mr. Singleton. They saw in you a man who could not be bought or frightened into approval, but whose strong moral stand made him a sucker for trickery. You've always felt the Four Clubs was the worst of possible methods of government. Hence, for you, change equals improvement. Can you think of anything worse than the four quarters of England at each other's throats all the time?"

"I suppose not," said Whitey uncertainly.

"What about the Four Clubs united under one banner, behaving and believing and being governed exactly as before, only now uniting all that hatred and blood-lust against a common enemy?"

Whitey laughed out loud.

"That's absurd."

Exsmith shrugged.

"You tell him, my dear."

"He's right, Whitey," said Hydrangea urgently. "Chaucer and Wildthorpe and the others are reckoning on a Continental war within five years."

"No," said Whitey.

"And your articles are a small part of their plans. Look Whitey," said Exsmith, using his first name for the first time in his effort to convince, "Britain wants back into Europe, but as the bully boy, not the prodigal son. In the last twenty years, who's emerged as the E.E.C.'s dominant member? Holland. Right. Unlikely as it seems, the Dutch dominate. They dictate the policies, they set the time. Only the Germans have vetoed the attempts of the Dutch to get Britain out. What makings of what an unholy alliance lie there!"

"This is pie in the sky," said Whitey. "This is vaguer than the weather forecast."

"Perhaps so," said Exsmith. "Perhaps not. How vague do you find these?"

He produced an envelope from an inside

pocket and from it took a series of photostatted typewritten sheets. The first of these was headed in bold black letters THE NEW ALBION.

"What's that mean?" asked Whitey. The words somehow filled him with foreboding.

"It means your new country," said Exsmith. "The phoenix that's going to rise from the ashes of the Four Clubs. Take a look."

Whitey began to read. When he finished he read it through again. It was allegedly the report of an Association working party on the proposed re-organization of the country. There was no hint in it of any change in approach or philosophy from the old Club structure.

"Not much space for democratic elections or the rule of law there," said Exsmith.

"Where did you get this?" asked Whitey.

"It's genuine, that's all you need to know. Mr. King I believe you've got something to contribute from your sources."

King handed over a loose roll of photostatted papers, about thirty closely handwritten sides.

"Wildthorpe's writing," he said. "You probably recognize it. His draft for a progress report and policy statement he'll be laying before the Association tomorrow. You get a couple of mentions yourself, Whitey. He's very complimentary about your usefulness. And your malleability."

Whitey said nothing, but read. It was true. He recognized the handwriting and as far as he could judge, it was Wildthorpe's. When he had finished, he handed the document back to King.

"It sounds bad," he admitted. "But men like these, Hobhouse and Wildthorpe, they've got to use the rhetoric of the Clubs to bind them together. Management has got to be convinced and it's terms like these which will do the convincing."

"You must be more stupid than you look!" exploded King, but Exsmith hushed the young man with a friendly pat on the shoulder.

"Whitey's right to examine what we say in a cool rational manner," he said. "His mistake is to try to separate the Directors from the Management. Take a look at this, Whitey. It's a photostat of an interrogation order. The capital M here means there's no limit on the techniques used. Hobhouse signed it, you notice. Now take a look at this photo."

"Oh Christ," said Whitey in revulsion. It was a naked man, or what was left of him. Something about the twisted, contorted features was familiar.

"Caldercote," he said, and could say no more.

"I'm afraid so. And there's something else which has just come to light. Your wife, Audrey. She didn't die in a London hospital. As soon as they thought of the substitute plan, they moved her right out of Athletic territory for the sake of security. She died in the sick bay at Wanderers Heights. They gave her treatment all right, to bring her round for questioning. Here's the authorization. Signed by Wildthorpe."

Whitey looked at the document without taking

any of it in. The words themselves were enough.

"Well," said King, the scornful edge now completely gone from his voice. "How do you fancy being a citizen of the New Albion, Whitey?"

Hydrangea glared angrily at the young man and put her arm protectively over Whitey's shoulders.

"Let's all have a drink," said Exsmith briskly, "and then we can talk things over."

After fifteen minutes and a couple of drinks, Whitey was ready for talking. Inside he still felt hollow. That Caldercote and Audrey were dead, even the manner of their deaths, had long been facts in his mind. Tonight they had ceased to be mere facts and had slipped from the mind into the imagination. He badly needed the reassurance of words to keep them at bay.

Exsmith spoke frankly.

"There's not much you as an individual can do. Even these articles you're writing are only a bit of window-dressing for the New Albion. Stop them and you achieve little. No, the thing is not to rock the boat just now. They are pretty convinced all they've got to worry about is breaking down the old parochial Club loyalties."

"What about the Jays?" interrupted Whitey.

"After tonight's meeting with Hydrangea, things will look hopeful for a rapprochement there," grinned King. "Over the next few weeks, we'll cautiously come together. Eventually they'll think we're their favourite nephews."

"So the thing is to keep everybody sweet," said Exsmith. "You're bound to pick up bits of useful information. This you can pass on. But no risks."

"So who *is* doing the work?" asked Whitey, feeling selfishly disgruntled at this further relegation into a minor role.

"The less you know the better," responded Exsmith, which didn't help his self-esteem either.

"At least tell me what the work is," demanded Whitey. "I've a right to know what my small contribution is being made *to*."

"I guess you're right," said Exsmith. "Our government concern is the balance of power in Europe."

"The *what?*" exclaimed Whitey, then laughed. "I haven't heard that phrase since my fourth form history lessons."

"Well, you're hearing it now. So, our short term objective is to prevent the Association from taking the first steps towards the New Albion. This we reckon can be done fairly easily by using the inter-Club distrust that already exists."

"Violently?" asked Whitey quietly.

"There may be some of the normal inter-Club violence, but that doesn't figure large in our plans. No, our sabotage will be done at the conference table."

"And the Jays?"

"We're going to do what we tried with Hydrangea at Coventry, only on a bigger scale," said King. "When the moment comes, enough evidence of the Association's collusion with the Underground will be released to discredit the whole of the Directorship."

"But what's in it for you?" asked Whitey. "Wouldn't you get more by sticking with the deal?"

"Whatever you think of us, Mr. Singleton, we don't see ourselves as storm-troopers for a fascist government," said King, suddenly angry. "This way, we stop something that needs stopping, and we open up the whole top level of government in this country. Naturally our friends, like Sheldrake, don't get tarred with the same brush as Hobhouse and the rest. After this lot, we should be able to start changing things from the top downwards. In fact, your way. So give us a smile, Whitey."

King's little flush of anger had gone and he had talked himself back to his former detached affability by the time he finished. Earlier he had phoned an enigmatic message from the flat and assured Whitey that the news would reach Sheldrake in half-an-hour that Singleton was no danger and arrangements would be put in train to paint the earlier events of the evening as a simple misunderstanding.

Hydrangea and the bearded man who seemed to be called Hort (short for what? wondered Whitey. Hortense?) contributed little to this discussion but sat and listened intently. Whitey wondered how much they too were hearing for the first time.

Finally Exsmith glanced at his watch.

"Late," he said. "I've got to go. We'll be in touch, Whitey. Stay with it, son. You can do both your countries a great service."

"I'll break too," said King. "Whitey, I shouldn't stray out till morning. Make sure Sheldrake's had time to get things sorted for you."

"But they'll know I haven't used my apartment tonight," protested Whitey.

"So? Tell them you bought yourself a bit of dressing-room comfort," laughed King.

The two men left together. Affability and frankness, thought Whitey, watching them go. Good qualities in a man. But this combination left him vaguely uneasy.

He turned to the other two and intercepted a glance between them.

"Secrets?" he asked.

Hort rose.

"I must be on my way too. Sorry I had to hit you, Singleton. Goodnight."

He went out, leaving Whitey touching his head. During the discussions he had forgotten the blow, but now the pain came back.

"And you?" he said to Hydrangea.

"I'm sorry, Whitey. About your wife. And your friend, Caldercote."

"Yes. Being associated with me seems to be a pretty dangerous business."

"Perhaps. I'd like to stay with you all the same, Whitey. If you want me to."

"Dressing-room comforts?" said Whitey with

an attempt at humour.

"Whatever you will."

"It would be kind," he said stiltedly.

This time, he thought, there would be no lurking doubts. Everyone knew everything he had to tell. As a source of information, he was bone-dry.

Nixon Lectures: Fifth Series

Documentary Material
1 (m) TEXT OF THE OFFICIAL ATHLETIC
SONG
(to the tune 'Onward Christian Soldiers')

Onward goes Athletic!
The greatest and the best!
Once you join Athletic
You soon forget the rest!
We are all Supporters
Young and old alike
Lead us into battle
We know when to strike!
Onward goes Athletic!
The greatest and the best!
Once you join Athletic
You soon forget the rest!

The following verse is a popular interpolation
Blue and green and yellow
Are all shades of shit!
There's just one true colour
And we're wearing it!
Red's the shade to show them!
Red from toe to head!
We'll kick them and we'll grind them
Till they're all bleeding red!
Onward goes Athletic!
etc.

Chapter 15

During the next month, Whitey found himself working surprisingly hard. Sheldrake had done the clearing-up job well and his return after the Parliament Hill business had been accepted almost without comment, to his face at least. The two dead Strikers had been written off as the results of a mutual misunderstanding in the excitement of the chase, an explanation which seemed to satisfy the Directors, though Whitey did not like the way some of the First Team looked at him as he walked around Athletic House.

His own public rehabilitation was almost complete. He had appeared before a Disciplinary Committee to have his case reviewed. All of them had been so well rehearsed in their lines that it had been rather like taking part in an amateur play production. In view of Whitey's full and frank recantation and his eagerness to return to the fold, the Committee agreed to suspend his sentence for a period of one year to test the sincerity of his reform.

Now he appeared frequently on the media networks, usually talking about the high regard in which England was held by most other countries and their regret that she did not play a greater role in the councils of the world. "What they would like," he said with vibrant sincerity looking the camera straight in the lens, "is to see a New Albion arise and take up its traditional role of leader and law-giver."

The 'New Albion' idea was soon being pushed everywhere and though Whitey knew his own contribution was relatively small, it still made him feel guilty. But there were moments when talking to Wildthorpe and Chaucer, even to Hobhouse, he could not believe that the black picture painted by Exsmith was true. From time to time as though sensing his doubts, Sheldrake (now very coldly correct in his relations with Whitey) edged him into a position from which he could see the underside of the whole business.

Part of the plan for uniting the Four Clubs depended on concentrating the attention of their Supporters Clubs on a common enemy. The glibs had been elected. For more than a decade the glibs had gone unmolested, as far as anyone had been able to go unmolested during this period of yussing and general licence. They had banded together into powerful groups of their own, some with a great deal of likeness to the more extreme Supporters Clubs, as Whitey had discovered to his cost. And these glib groups paid little allegiance to the Club in whose territory they existed but, paradoxically, provided one of the few existing forms of the national unity which the Association now desired. It was this which made them the perfect target. Club fervour could be used as the starting point for the persecution, but quickly the fever spread across Club boundaries, and soon in the border territories groups of red and blue and yellow and green favours were mingling in common lynch mobs.

Sheldrake unobtrusively arranged for Whitey to be present in an operations centre one evening. At first he did not understand what was happening, but quickly he began to catch on.

A bunch of about thirty glibs rounded up in London had been brought to north Cambridgeshire, allegedly for internment. But arrangements had been made for them to escape. A couple of trucks had been temptingly positioned, inviting theft, and the road north was the only one left open. The local Supporters Clubs were informed and assistance requested. The trucks, each fitted with a hidden signal device which let the men in the control room know their exact position, were carefully shepherded north. A message was sent across the border into Wanderers territory in Lincolnshire inviting them to join in the chase. The ambush was sprung near Spalding, one truck was wrecked and taken but the other got away and headed west, weaving back and forth between Wanderers and Athletic territory and closely pursued by local Strikers from both Clubs. Finally the truck crashed near Uppingham, the glibs took to the fields and their pursuers converged upon them in a united mopping up operation.

The following morning Sheldrake told the protesting Whitey that afterwards the two sets of

Supporters had a small celebration, with lots of booze, mutual backslapping, exchange of colours. A great success.

Glib-hunting soon became a major political weapon in more ways than one. The Directors used the hatred so engendered to get rid of anyone in the Club hierarchy they felt might be opposed to their plans. There were many of these, men whose loyalty to the Club could never be sublimated into support for the re-unified nation. They would go home at night to find their houses strewn with all the paraphernalia of glibdom. And a mob would arrive within a couple of minutes.

Old scores too were easily settled thus and Whitey himself came dangerously close to being yussed out of existence. As he opened his flat door one night, he was seized from behind by two men and flung to the ground. Other men trampled over him into the flat and after a few seconds he was dragged to his feet and half carried into the lounge.

There were half a dozen men in there, triumphantly displaying articles of female clothing and cosmetics.

"We were told about you, you reffing glib," said their obese leader gleefully. "Think you can come back here and be treated like the prodigal reffing son, do you? Prodigal reffing daughter, more like!"

The others laughed. They were, Whitey decided looking at them as closely as his dazed condition permitted, they were genuine glib-hunters, rather than Strikers seeking a pretence for killing him. Except the fat man who was in charge. He looked as if he was in on the plant; something in his expression suggested calculation rather than blood-lust.

"Those clothes aren't mine," said Whitey.

"Bloody right they're not!" guffawed the fat man. "Why do you wear them then?"

"I don't wear them," said Whitey, concentrating his attention on the other men. His only hope lay in producing some rational evidence that the clothes were a plant. "Look, call the Management. Let me ring Athletic House. They'll vouch for me there."

"No reffing doubt," said the fat man quickly. "They've been weeding the glibs out of there like fluff from an Eskimo's belly button. Oh yes, they'll vouch for you, duckie. Let's get it over, boys."

"For Christ's sake," yelled Whitey as the men began to advance on him rather hesitantly. "Just take a look at those clothes. Hold them up! They're made for a small woman; how the hell do you think I'd get into them?"

This was rational all right. It was also the wrong thing to say.

"Don't its clothes fit then?" mocked the fat man to the accompaniment of laughter from the others. "Is it putting on weight? Well, we're the boys to take it off you, aren't we, lads?"

That was it. The stimulus to action had been

given and accepted. There was no hesitancy now.

"Wait, wait!" screamed Whitey. "For God's sake wait!"

"Yes," said a new voice. "I think it would be a good idea to wait."

Everyone froze, then looked round. Standing in the bathroom door was Hydrangea. She was wearing Whitey's bath robe. It trailed on the ground round her feet and the sleeves were a foot too long. She looked very small and helpless.

"What's going on?" she said. "Whitey, love, who are these men?"

"They say I'm a glib," he answered.

"A glib?" She laughed incredulously. "If he's a glib, he's got some funny ideas, I can tell you!"

One or two of the men smiled uncertainly and she pressed home her advantage.

"What are you doing with my clothes? You'll ruin them treating them like that!"

First one, then another of the intruders draped the garments they were holding carefully over chair-backs.

The fat man came back to life.

"Come on, lads! Don't be taken in. Find one and you'll find a nest. You've all seen these things on the street. What makes you think this isn't another wearing the full strip?"

This notion pulled the men up short for a moment, but Hydrangea was ready for them.

She moved her left arm from in front of her body and the robe fell open.

"Satisfied?" she enquired ironically.

231

Sheepishly the men began to make for the door, a couple of them even muttering semi-audible apologies to Whitey as they passed.

"Don't leave it at this, lads!" yelled the fat man. "You're being fooled. Don't you see it?"

"Too reffing well," rejoined one of his followers, glancing at Hydrangea.

The fat man relaxed as though accepting defeat and joined the trek to the doorway. But as he passed Whitey, he swept a short thick-bladed knife from his tunic pocket and made a surprisingly swift lunge at his stomach. Taken by surprise the most Whitey could do was take a short step backwards which fetched him up against the wall. The fat man drew back the knife for a second try. There was an ear-cracking explosion whose echoes were drowned by a full, high scream of pain from the fat man. He fell forward against Whitey, but the knife had dropped to the floor where it stuck deep in the carpet with the handle vibrating gently.

In the bathroom door Hydrangea was standing with her right arm outstretched. In the dangling end of the overlong sleeve was a smoking hole from which protruded the dull metal snout of a pistol. She no longer looked small and helpless.

"You can go now," she said. "Help him through the door, Whitey."

The gunshot had sent the other men fleeing in panic down the outside corridor. Whitey could hear their hasty footsteps receding down the stairwell.

"He's hurt," said Whitey unnecessarily. The fat man was bleeding copiously from the shoulder. Hydrangea reached into the bathroom, plucked a towel from the rail and flung it over.

"That'll stop you bleeding on the landing," she said. "Now get out!"

With the towel pressed hard against his wound, the fat man staggered through the door towards the stairs. Whitey watched him go with some concern, till Hydrangea came up behind him and kicked the door shut.

"You start getting too worried about animals," she said, "and you end up leaving your money to a cat's home. Are you hurt?"

"No. Just shaken. Thanks."

He went back into the lounge, picked up some of the garments and examined them.

"These aren't yours?" he said.

"Certainly not. I've got *some* taste. No, you've been planted Whitey. Lucky I was here."

"Yes. How long had you been?"

"About half an hour. This lot must have been tucked nicely away in your wardrobe and drawers. I noticed nothing at first. I helped myself to a shower and was just getting dried when you and your friends came."

"Lucky you take your gun into the shower with you," said Whitey ironically.

"Wasn't it? I hoped to sort things out without using it, but Fatso was here to get rid of you, come what may."

"Who do you think set this up?" asked Whitey,

pouring them both a stiff Scotch. As his new status became established, his access to the little luxuries of life had been made easier too. He enjoyed them, perhaps too much, he thought uneasily.

"God knows. Not everyone loves you, but you've become important enough now to make an official yussing difficult. A glib-lynch, that's different."

He tried to pull her down on to his knee but she evaded him saying, 'later'. They had seen a lot of each other in the past few weeks. Hydrangea's rise to favour had been almost as meteoric as Whitey's and she was now firmly established as a kind of p.a. to Chaucer who was spending a great deal of time in London at the moment. She and Whitey made no secret of their relationship. Its background was well known to the Directors and it made a perfect cover for meetings at which they could exchange information. But to Whitey at least it had become a great deal more than a cover.

"Anything new?" he asked her. She nodded towards the bathroom as she answered, "Not much."

"I think I'll grab a shower," he said, standing up. "Freshen my drink and bring it in, love."

He was not sure of the extent to which his flat was bugged, but he took no chances. While it was eerily unpleasant to think of someone listening in on their love-making, at least the results weren't going to be fatal. Business discussions always took place in the shower.

As he stepped under the tepid water (gratefully; often there was no water at all) he wondered what the distant eavesdroppers would have made of the attempt to yuss him.

Hydrangea joined him. They kissed and clung close.

"Two showers in half an hour. You'll be washed away to nothing."

"I doubt it," said Hydrangea looking down disgruntedly at her well made body. She was finding it difficult to withstand the onslaught of the starch-rich diet which was the common fare of the people.

"What's new?" asked Whitey.

"Things are going too well," she said. "What no-one reckoned on are the norms. Everyone talks about silent majorities, but no-one really believes in them. Well, it's becoming clear that the Four Clubs problem is nothing like as difficult as it seemed. The norms want to live in a unified country. For a decade now the ordinary man's been in a position where if he didn't join a Supporters Club, nominally at least, he was in real trouble. And to express anything less than loyalty-to-the death to your Club meant that even your own family would yuss you. But the change in atmosphere that the Directors have been contriving has turned things upside down. You know what happened yesterday in Oxford? A band of the local citizenry yussed an assole procession! Christ, only a couple of weeks ago, anyone who saw that lot trotting down the street dived for cover."

"Yes indeed," said Whitey thoughtfully, remembering his own experiences in the city. "And this is happening all over?"

"It seems so."

"Well, that's not bad, is it? I mean, if the ordinary people can reassert themselves, perhaps this is a way of killing the Clubs and the New Albion at the same time."

She drew away from him and looked at him pityingly.

"You're too idealistic for your own good, Whitey. The norms aren't idealistic at all. What they want is peace and prosperity. How it comes, they don't care. They'll accept anything that promises these things. If the New Albion means there's going to be food in the shops, water in the pipes, dustcarts in the streets and some kind of law in the courts, it'll have their unqualified support."

"It's not a bad deal," said Whitey, shivering as the temperature of the shower dropped from tepid to cold.

"You think not? I expect you'll be glad to hear that the Dutch have lost their motion to expel us from the E.E.C. Renewed prosperity begins to loom, eh? I expect you'll be glad to hear too that there have been secret talks between the Directors and the Germans and everyone comes out looking very happy. That the proportion of diplomats to military advisers in the German Embassy at the moment is something like one to three. I daresay you'll be delighted to hear that we're running out of glibs to persecute and that they're turning their attention to coloureds in the Midlands."

She was shouting and Whitey put his hand over her mouth as the water from the shower died to a trickle. She bit his fingers viciously.

"Christ!" he said and slapped her backside with all his strength. Angrily she turned to go but he grabbed her shoulders and pulled her back. They wrestled for a moment till Whitey trod on the soap and his feet skidded away from under him.

He hit the tiled floor with a thump that knocked all the breath out of him.

"You all right?" asked Hydrangea anxiously.

He didn't answer and she knelt beside him. Quickly he grabbed and pulled her across his body.

"If the lecture's over," he said, "you can tell me all about it. Are you sitting comfortably?"

"You could call it that," she answered smiling. "No, the thing is this, Whitey. Our disruption programme is not going too well. Like I said, it's been a surprise to everyone how much momentum the New Albion movement's picked up. The kind of thing we've been doing has been mere pinpricks. And the Directors' personal Strikers have been weeding out a lot of operatives, King's and ours too. I don't think we're the only ones who've infiltrated the enemy."

"That's dangerous," said Whitey, suddenly very worried. "If they capture someone who knows the whole set up . . ."

"Aha!" said Hydrangea, smiling. "Now you know what Sheldrake felt like when they took you!"

"Surprisingly enough," answered Whitey, "it was you I was worrying about."

It wasn't wholly true. Perfect altruism is only possible in action, never in thought. But it won him a passionate embrace.

"So what's the plan?" he asked finally.

"God knows. I'm too small a cog. But I gather it centres upon disrupting the Wembley Rally. That's too public for any trouble to be hushed up."

"Disrupting it," he repeated. The phrase was too smooth, too pat. It made him feel uneasy. "But how?"

"All will be revealed no doubt. It's getting reffing cold in here. Let's go to bed and give the boys on listening duty something to gossip about."

The Wembley Rally was planned as the central public festival of the re-unification movement. Wembley had been chosen because, despite its obvious association with Athletic during the reign of the Four Clubs, it still retained much of its old image as the national stadium, belonging to no particular club.

A grand parade was planned, a mingling of

238

contingents from all the Clubs, accompanied by music, dancing, displays, speeches, and leading to two days of general holiday and carnival. The Wembley Rally would be mirrored at stadia up and down the whole country, while those not wishing or not able to attend would be able to watch the whole thing on private or public tele-screens.

Whitey was officially involved here. The huge television studio built under the roof at Wembley in the early eighties was to act as the centre of operations. Whitey had been given the job of interviewing the party of foreign dignitaries who were attending the Rally. They were mostly European, though Exsmith was invited also, and Whitey's task was to bring out their love of and respect for England, and their desire to see her wholly back in the E.E.C.

His task as described to him by King was rather different.

"We'll have a lot of our boys planted in the crowd," he explained. "They'll stir up a bit of trouble, work on old inter-Club quarrels, that kind of thing. It shouldn't be difficult."

"People could get hurt," objected Whitey.

"So there'll be a few bloody noses and even a cracked head or two. For God's sake, Whitey, we can't just wave banners and sing songs."

"All right," said Whitey dubiously. "Where do I come in."

"Well, that t.v. studio's going to be pretty closely checked. But it's essential that we have somebody in there when the trouble starts. We need to let the tele-viewers see what's going on — this has got to be national, not just a bit of bother in north London. Also we want someone to let the people know just what has been going on behind their backs."

"So you want me to take over the t.v. studio?" asked Whitey incredulously.

"No! We don't want you blown. Our own man will be at the reception beforehand, Sheldrake's arranged that. But he won't leave when the other's go to take their seats for the Rally.

"That's where you come in. You'll be rehearsing there before the day. Your job is to find somewhere for our man to hide so that the Strikers won't find him when they check that everyone's left. And we want you to leave this in the hiding place."

This was a machine-pistol with two full clips.

"What's this for?" demanded Whitey.

"Look, how do you think our man's going to persuade those technicians to do what he wants? By rational argument? No, he needs a weapon. And those reffing Strikers won't be letting anybody with weapons into the Studio that night. Not even Management. So the things got to be hidden there beforehand."

Whitey examined the plan thoughtfully.

"Who does the talk-to-the-people bit?" he asked.

"It's on video-tape," answered King. "No sweat."

"And your man, does he know there's no chance of getting out alive. Once they realize what's going on, there'll be Strikers all over the place."

"Once he's dealt with the couple who stay inside the Studio, he'll be fine," answered King. "Those doors will stand anything less than an h.e. shell. He'll have plenty of time."

"And afterwards?"

King shrugged.

"He knows the risk. And don't be worried that he'll give anything away. He's got a set of dentures so full of cyanide that if he bit an elephant, it would drop dead."

Whitey shuddered.

"All right," he said. "Let's talk details."

But his mind was cloudy with unease as they talked deep into the night. And though nothing that was said then or in the weeks that followed gave substance to his unease, the Wembley Rally began to loom in his mind like a festival of disaster. But for whom, he could not guess.

Nixon Lectures: Fifth Series

Audio-Visual Material

5 **(y)** Extract from tape of pre-trial interrogation of Whitey Singleton (1992). Quality poor, but text authenticated by Whitey Singleton.

Interrogator:	You feeling all right now?
Singleton:	Oh Christ.
Interrogator:	Look, I don't like this either. I've got to go home and have dinner with my wife and kids.
Singleton:	Try . . . bring . . . them . . . for . . . late show.
Interrogator:	Names, that's what we want. We know who they are, your terrorist friends. We just want confirmation. To protect the innocent.
Singleton:	No names. Just me. Reporter. Anti-violence.
Interrogator:	Yes, but you incite others, don't you see that? Anyway, do you say that you wouldn't join in an act of violence against the Club?
Singleton:	No.
Interrogator:	No, you don't say that?
Singleton:	No, I wouldn't.
Interrogator:	And you wouldn't encourage an act of violence?
Singleton:	No.
Interrogator:	Or condone such an act later?

	Even if you approved.
Singleton.	No!
Interrogator:	I think I'll go and have my dinner. You're either too clever or too stupid for me.

Chapter 16

Whitey intended to arrive at Wembley with an hour or more to spare, but he reckoned without the crowds. For half a mile around the Stadium the streets were jammed solid with people and it rapidly became clear they were not moving. The reason for the jam was easy to deduce from the huge tele-screens which dominated every street. Wembley Stadium was packed to capacity and had been for over two hours. The crowds outside were amazingly good-humoured, apparently content enough with their physical proximity to the stadium and the excellent tele-pictures they were getting of the interior. All over the country, the excited commentators announced, people were gathering to view their screens, and many parallel ceremonies were being held at the famous football grounds throughout the provinces.

There was no hope of getting through by car. Any vehicle on the streets was soon forced to come to a halt and almost immediately it was taken over as a vantage point from which to view the nearest screen.

Whitey retreated rapidly and for a while believed that he was not going to be able to get through at all. But others were in a similar position and when he contacted the Television Centre, he discovered a heli-lift had been organized from Wood Lane. Even getting there proved difficult and he was last aboard the last of the three 'copters which were being used.

The scene as they dropped down into the bowl of Wembley was almost impossible for the mind to take in. Whitey had seen the place packed before, at international football matches when he was a boy, and later for Athletic Supporters' rallies. But this was the first time he had had an aerial view and also, he was certain, the first time scenes such as these had taken place.

For a start everywhere was covered with people. Inside and out. Great surges could be seen in the crowds surrounding the stadium so that it was like looking down on an ocean in storm. The slanting oval roof of the stadium itself had been invaded by spectators who waved and screamed and hurled streamers at the helicopter as it sank slowly past them. It was like dropping into a funnel of people, a Dantesque concept which did nothing for Whitey's peace of mind.

As the helicopter dropped lower, the sound came at them from all sides, tangibly, almost visibly, so that the roar of the racing engine was taken over, smothered and finally incorporated in the roar of the crowd, too multifarious for harmony but too solid for discord. It merely *was*.

The Stadium was built to hold a hundred thousand people. Tonight it must have been overcrowded by at least twenty per cent. The double crash barrier, the twenty-foot electrified fence, and the concrete moat, which provided the three circles of defence round the pitch, looked puny, child's construction-kit things to set against these cliffs of human beings which soared away from Whitey's awestruck gaze.

As he jumped from the helicopter, he stumbled and fell forward, putting one hand to the ground. The turf felt warm and resilient. This was it, he suddenly realized. Wembley. The famous playing surface which had figured large in every school-boy's dreams fifteen years ago. Now he was on it.

And out there, on the terraces, crushed and frightened perhaps despite the comfort of their fathers' presence, were schoolboys to whom this was a place of pure mythology, like the new Greeks who were still awed by Mount Olympus but had never seen the gods.

Looking round the walls of spectators, he was filled with a tremendous love for them, a desire to serve, and at the same time with a desperate sense of foreboding.

"Papers?" demanded a Striker who had come forward to the helicopter. Whitey produced his identification which was scrutinized with meticulous care before he was allowed to move on. Three more times he had to convince progressively more disbelieving officials of his identity and submit to an obtrusively intimate search, before he was permitted to enter the lift and ascend to the television studio which nestled against the stadium roof. 'Nestled' was perhaps not the right word. It was a large structure, made to seem fairly small in relation to the stadium itself but very extensive internally.

Security requirements might be very strict, but there were plenty of people able to satisfy them, thought Whitey as he entered and looked around. It was not quite as crowded in here as it had been outside, but there were still more people within than the reception area could comfortably hold. He wondered which of them was King's man but quickly dismissed the speculation. He wouldn't be wearing a lapel-badge. The red light shone above the Studio door and through the glass panel he saw that Hobhouse, Wildthorpe, Mervyn of City and Leary of United were being interviewed. These men had come more and more into the foreground of recent weeks. The Club managers were too well known, had too long been set up as infamous bogeymen in neighbouring territories, to be readily acceptable at this stage. So the four major directors had begun to appear, still identifiable as fit and able representatives of their respective Clubs but with none of the psychological overtones. It was possible to believe in a Club union negotiated by these men.

Whitey made his way to the control room where his presence was acknowledged with a harassed nod. He examined the bank of monitors. The picture Stan Linley, the producer, was presently using was a close-up of Wildthorpe who was talking in a blunt, earnest, forthright way which he'd been rehearsing for weeks about the joy all true Englishmen felt on this great occasion. "We've been Four Clubs and nothing else for too long," he averred staring frankly into the camera. "Tonight we don't stop being Four Clubs. No. That would be daft. But we become members of one greater club under one banner with one loyalty. To the New Albion."

As he spoke these last two or three sentences Linley, a brisk rather smooth young man, faded in a section of the spectators across which the camera tracked showing clearly the various colours, yellow, green, red, blue, still mainly segregated, but everywhere, transcending the Club barriers, was the lily white of the New Albion. The crowd was chanting now, or rather not so much chanting as calling, singing almost, the three syllables of Albion, drawing each out to a greater length, setting up a bell-like reverberation around the stadium.

"When do I do my bit, Stan?" asked Whitey.

"Christ knows, Whitey. The wogs have all been held up by the crowds, they're trying to get them in by helicopter, but it means scouting round every bloody Embassy. Silly load of wankers. Let's have a great big close-up of Wildthorpe in a moment. Then pull back to show them all. But would someone on the floor tell Hobhouse his nose is running? Yes. Quick as you can. Do you think the old bastard will have a hanky? By the way, Whitey, the Yanks won't be coming."

"What?"

"Yes. So it'll just be our European chums. Better, I think. You can invite them all to be subtly nasty about Uncle Sam. Well, tell him to use his sleeve!"

"Why aren't they coming?" asked Whitey.

"God knows. Some little diplomatic tiff, no doubt."

"No doubt."

Or more than that. Perhaps word of the plan had got to the Directors and Exsmith had decided to stick to the safety of his Embassy. Christ! how did it come about that the best the combined mights of the U.S. of A. and the Jays could produce was something as weak as this?

Then another thought struck him. If the Directors *had* got wind of the plan, then perhaps their source had provided them with other information. About himself. Hardly likely or he'd be undergoing a short sharp yussing now. Or about Hydrangea. Chaucer he'd noticed in the crowd. But the girl had not been with him.

"Give me a call if I'm on," he said casually and stepped out of the control room.

Back in the reception area, a move for the doors was beginning. Whitey glanced at his watch. Official kick-off time was eight P.M. and it was five minutes to now. The V.I.P.s would be returning to their seats in the old Royal Box.

He made for the door and buttonholed Chaucer as he passed. He had seen little of the Wanderers manager in recent weeks and Chaucer did not seem overjoyed at the brief reunion.

"Hydrangea here?" he asked as casually as he could.

"What? No. I thought you'd have been knocking her off all day as usual and you'd come together. Perhaps she's found someone else."

Chaucer pushed by with a short laugh at his own wit. But Whitey thought he detected something else there. A hidden knowledge. Or was he becoming paranoically sensitive?

It was beginning to dawn on Whitey that another face was missing. Sheldrake's. He could see him nowhere. There was a chance that he might have returned to his seat while Whitey was in the control room, but he could not recall noticing him on first entry either.

This made things worse. One of the two missing would have been a source of faint worry. But both added up almost to certainty.

"Do you have a light?" asked a swarthy young man in a black tunic. His voice was thin and nasal and Whitey guessed he came from City territory.

"Sorry," said Whitey, turning away. He felt his arm grasped.

"In that case, perhaps you could help me find one," murmured the swarthy man. "Mr. King said you might be able to help."

Whitey had forgotten about King's T.V. expert for the moment and viewed him now as an unnecessary distraction from the important business of worrying about Hydrangea.

Quickly he led him to a quiet corner.

"Look," he said in a low voice. "I smell trouble. Exsmith's not here, I think at least part of the plan's been blown."

"But not my part it would seem, friend," observed the man, unmoved. "So take me to wherever we're going."

"What's the point?" demanded Whitey.

"Just take me."

Something in the swarthy man's voice made Whitey obey. He led him towards the control room, then down a short corridor to the make-up room. If this fool wanted to risk his life, that was his look-out. Except, of course, that he knew all about Whitey. The thought pulled him up short for a moment, then he dismissed it. If King said his man was ready to take the suicide pill or whatever it was, that was good enough. No, his major concern at the moment was to find a way of getting out of the stadium. With a sinking heart he remembered the huge crowds outside. Even if he could bluff his way past the guardian Strikers, it would take him hours to get through the press of people. The delay would be fatal both to flight or to any rescue attempt on Hydrangea. He was uncertain which came first.

He opened the make-up door and peered in. As he'd anticipated the girl was down on the studio floor doing running repairs to the interviewees. He opened another door.

"This is the costume cupboard," he said. He took the machine-pistol out of the arm of an ancient great-coat, kept here for God knew what purpose. "The girl shouldn't have cause to go in there."

The swarthy man shrugged.

"Let's hope she stays lucky," he said flatly.

Whitey returned to the reception room which was emptying rapidly. The light above the studio door was green and as he watched, the door opened and the Directors filed out.

Wildthorpe spotted him and came across.

"How are you doing, son? You've been working well, I hear. It won't be forgotten, never you fear. Are you coming out to see the fun?"

"No, I'd better stay here. I'm supposed to be talking to the Europeans when they arrive," answered Whitey. Wildthorpe too sounded genuinely friendly. Could he act like this if something were suspected? More important, what would be the point?

The Director laughed.

"That lot! You needn't bother. They're coming in by chopper. We'll let them see what a real Albion welcome is. They'll be shitting garlic! We'll take 'em straight to their seats, so you'll have to do your chat a bit later. OK? Come on then."

He put his arm round Whitey's shoulders and led him out of the now empty room. The door was slammed shut behind them by two Strikers. They entered the lift which did not take them right down to pitch level but stopped halfway. They stepped out on to a concrete stair-landing. Another door straight ahead opened into the heat

252

of the main stand and as they stepped out into the open air, they felt the noise of the crowd break over them like water.

Wildthorpe drew Whitey with him into the Royal Box, ignoring his protests.

"Always room for my friends," he said. "Them frogs arrived yet?"

"No, Mr. Wildthorpe. Another ten minutes at least, so they say."

"Right," said Wildthorpe to the young aide who had spoken.

"Can't wait any longer. Let's get this show on the road. The heli-pilot can hold them above the Stadium till the entrance parade's done. Serve the sods right. Off you go and press the starter, son."

The aide left and Wildthorpe grinned at Whitey.

"Creepy little wanker, that one. You can have his seat."

Whitey sat down. There was nothing else to do. He was trapped in the Stadium as firmly as if he had been in Wormwood Scrubs. More firmly, perhaps. He'd been able to get out of the Scrubs.

"Right," said Wildthorpe. "Everyone sitting comfortably? Then we'll begin."

His timing was excellent. As he finished, from each corner of the Stadium in turn a broad shaft of coloured lights tumefied into the air, red, green, yellow, blue. The columns swung and swayed, collided and crossed, till finally they focussed at a common apex, high above the centre of the pitch; and immediately from other parts of the Stadium sharp-edged shafts of brilliant white light were hurled to join them, till a four sided pyramid was formed. This was the signal for thousands of multi-coloured balloons to be released from the concrete moat which ran round the ground. For a few moments the air was full of the bobbing, soaring, luminescent shapes, then they passed through the walls of light and were gone.

The crowd 'oohed' its appreciation; music sounded; first a fanfare amplified sufficiently to penetrate the noise even of such a gathering as this, then a rapid stirring military march. And into the arena from their respective corners trotted teams of Supporters from the Four Clubs. Their banners waved, their colours shone brilliantly, as they converged on the centre of the pitch. It looked as if a collision were inevitable and the cries from the crowd were becoming increasingly partisan. But just as the front lines, locked together with linked arms, reached each other, they released their grips and split into files, running lines of blue, green, red and yellow together in a pattern at first simple but becoming more and more intricate as the trotters swirled and threaded their way round the pitch. In the end Whitey found he had lost the concept of them as individuals and was now viewing them purely as living lines of colour, like a cartoonist's animation or the contents of a gently shaken kaleidoscope.

Now from the central tunnel poured a new

stream of trotters, girls this time, wearing tight fitting track-suits in pure white. More and more of them poured out in an unbroken line till they filled the track round the pitch. Next they converged on the central whirl of colour, pressing in on it, shaping, moulding.

For a moment it looked as if something had gone wrong, the patterns seemed broken, unbalanced. Then the shapes began to make sense and applause broke out in the crowd, swelling to a climax of hand-clapping, foot-stamping, whistling and cheering as more and more of the spectators spotted the word spelled out by the multi-coloured blocks in the plain of white.

ALBION.

"The buggers should have a good view of that," said Wildthorpe with satisfaction, looking up into the tent of light. Whitey followed his gaze. Looking as if it were perched on the pinnacle of light was a helicopter containing, he presumed, the foreign dignitaries.

The martial music had stopped. Wildthorpe rose to his feet and all over the Stadium others followed suit. The Anthem, thought Whitey. But which? They could hardly single out one of the Club songs. Perhaps the old standard 'God save our gracious team' would be sung. But this too had local, limited associations for each individual Supporter.

Wildthorpe held a printed song sheet in front of him.

"We'll have a proper anthem later, of course," he said. "But for the time being and for this occasion especially, it was a toss-up between Blake's 'Jerusalem' and this. I think it's the right choice. Don't you?"

Whitey looked in amazement as the band struck up.

This was the hymn 'Abide with me.'

The crowd began to sing.

Suddenly Whitey recalled the first Cup Final he had ever seen; aged seven, his arms wrapped firmly round his dad's neck, his dad's firm slightly flat baritone voice sounding these words in his ear.

Help of the helpless, O abide with me.

The tradition of singing this hymn at Cup Finals had died in the early seventies, but there were obviously plenty of older Supporters for whom singing it now would be a nostalgic and unifying experience.

Change and decay in all around I see

And the dirge-like tune, the morbid sentimentality of the words, these were just the things to bring a collective self-gratulatory lump to the mob's throat and soothe its savage breast.

I fear no foe, with Thee at hand to bless

Whitey looked at Wildthorpe who was singing loudly and smiling benevolently at the crowd at the same time. Did he imagine he was the *thee* of the hymn?

Where is death's sting? Where, grave, thy victory?

In the stand opposite there seemed to be some

kind of disturbance, difficult to spot through the dazzling curtain of light or to fully hear through the singing of a hundred thousand voices. But a sense of movement was given and an edge of discord cut into the hymn. Wildthorpe's smile was troubled for a moment, but not very troubled.

He must have been expecting some bother, thought Whitey. He was a realist. No doubt the crowds were full of Strikers ready to pounce on trouble-makers. It was going to take more than a few protesters, no matter how well drilled, to disturb these proceedings. Another damp squib from Exsmith and King.

Hold Thou Thy cross before my closing eyes;

Somewhere close by there was an explosion, followed by the chatter of small arms fire. In the Royal Box the singing died away as the Directors looked at each other in consternation. Elsewhere in the stands others, further removed from the source and probably taking it for the beginnings of the firework display programmed for later in the evening, continued the song.

Shine through the gloom and point me to the skies;
Heaven's morning breaks . . .

And it did. From somewhere behind the main stand, a rocket stabbed into the sky and exploded into a myriad bright and blazing lights. But the trajectory of the rocket was not the easy parabola of a firework, and the explosion was the simple, incredible destruction of the helicopter carrying the foreign dignitaries. It, or what remained of it, became a ball of fire which plunged to earth outside the stadium though its hectic aura could still be plainly seen above the grandstand roof.

For a moment there was a shocked, incredulous silence. Then chaos. Whitey had time to see the multicoloured letters of ALBION painted on the sea of white waver, break up, dissolve; time to notice also how the colours ran in all directions for a second, then quickly reformed in blocks of yellow and green and blue and red; and time for nothing more but survival.

The whole of Wembley was embattled. Everywhere sounded shrieks of rage, of terror, of pain; flashes of gun-fire burnt violet holes in the darkness, momentarily illumining hordes of people so densely packed that even their struggles seemed static.

Up here in the Royal Box it was almost possible to think of it as a mere spectacle. It can't be happening, thought Whitey. It can't be. What's gone wrong?

Then Hobhouse, three seats away, suddenly twisted violently and fell, half of his head missing.

After that there was no thought of being spectators.

Whitey gave up conscious choice of direction in the next five minutes and concentrated on keeping his feet as he was swept down the steps which led to the pitch. So great was the pressure of bodies that it became almost impossible to inflate the lungs and he had to fight for a few inches of breathing space. From time to time through the din of the crowd and the crash of gunfire he heard other, different, cracking noises. They came from the crash-barriers surrounding the pitch, which were snapping like lengths of balsa-wood under the thrust and drive of the terrified crowd. Beyond them, the electrified fence was swept aside like misty gossamer and the first wave of spectators plunged into the concrete moat. It was seven-foot deep. Panic might well have given them the strength to drag themselves out on to the comparative safety of the pitch, but there was no time. Wave after wave followed till the moat was filled with bodies, live, dead, and dying, making a bridge over which those behind passed without awareness of, or care for, what they were treading on.

This was the moment of the night which remained for ever with Whitey. To the nightmare of the small boy in the burning coach was now added this new terror of running, running, running across a soft, yielding, heaving, screaming mass of human flesh.

But the nightmare came later. Now it was just a necessary part of survival. Once on the pitch, though the crowds were still dense, some element of free choice of movement returned. Grimly he began to force his way towards the lift shaft which led to the television studio. To reach it he had to go down the tunnel to the changing rooms area and this was so packed with spectators seeking an escape route that it required an act of will to abandon the starry vastness of the open sky and enter. Fortunately the greater part of those passing through were concerned merely with getting clear away from the Stadium, not with exploring its unknown areas. Whitey, remembering the thousands of people already waiting outside, did not envy anyone who got through the exit.

He ignored the lift and began to ascend the stairs. He had wondered briefly as he was swept by it why no-one in the Royal Box had tried to go through the door high in the stand which led to the studio lift. When he reached the landing, he saw why. The door had been barred from the inside. Several large pieces of studio equipment had been pushed against it. And whether as extra weight or merely for ease of disposal, a pile of bodies had been thrown on to the landing also. They were mostly Strikers, but not all. Near the top of the heap, open-eyed but clearly lifeless, was Stan Linley.

Sick to the heart, he rounded the corner. A gun exploded and a bullet flattened itself against the wall behind him. His eyes registered two armed men by the studio door before he fell back under cover.

"Hold it," he heard himself screaming. "I'm Singleton. Singleton. Check with . . ."

He tailed off, realizing he did not know the swarthy man's name. But after only a brief pause a familiar voice called, "Whitey? You there? Come on up. Slowly now."

He stepped round the corner. Standing at the

head of the stairs, smiling welcomingly, was King.

Inside the studio, all was calm, the only movement being in the control room where the TV personnel, looking white and strained, were working steadily and efficiently under the swarthy man's direction.

Whitey collapsed on a chair in the reception area and gratefully took the drink which King offered.

"For Christ's sake," he demanded, "what's happening? What's gone wrong?"

King looked at him thoughtfully.

"I'm never sure about you, Whitey. Do you really not know? I doubt it. I think there's part of you that doesn't *want* to know, but you're too bright not to have guessed long ago. Nothing's gone wrong. This is what we've been planning for weeks."

"Planning? *This?* But why?"

"Come into the control room."

The swarthy man waved at him as at an old friend, but Whitey ignored him staring at the monitors. The remote control cameras set all around the stadium were swooping and boring into the crowd, ignoring the panic-stricken majority but picking out hand-to-hand fights and gun-battles between different coloured factions.

"There now," said King proudly. "All over the country, those not actually fighting are seeing this. We've taken over all the regional tele-stations too, so that we're putting out a different commentary for each Club. Down here, naturally, it's rather biased towards Athletic. I'd wear your reds tonight."

He led Whitey from the control room and sat him before a viewing screen.

"Want to watch?"

"No. Jesus, *no!* Why are you doing this?"

"Obvious, I should have thought. The Four Clubs achieved a stasis. On this the Directors hoped to build the New Albion. We've pushed things back to the Four Club state, and beyond. They're going to destroy themselves by warfare and this time *we're* going to move in and pick up the pieces."

He looked like a man who had just produced a perfectly reasonable plan for a new system of traffic control.

"You're mad," said Whitey. "What can you hope for? You'll have all of Europe around your ears. And Exsmith, what do you think Exsmith is going to do when he sees what's happening?"

"Yes, killing off that chopper-load of Euros wasn't really planned. We thought they'd be in the ground already," said King thoughtfully. Then he cheered up. "But never fret yourself about Exsmith, your dear ambassador. Oh no. All this, well most of it, was his idea!"

Nixon Lectures : Fifth Series

Documentary Material

1 (s) Extract from letter received (May 1990) by U.S. citizen of British extraction from his 74-year-old father living in one of England's major industrial cities. (N.B. Italicised passages were expunged by the English Postal Censorship Office, but reinstated through our infra-red techniques.)

Things here could be worse. *Some weeks I can't get my pension,* but things have been better since your nephew joined what they call the First Team. He's a good lad and sees me OK *though some of his mates are a rough lot. Old Joe Burton told one of them to sod off the other day and was lucky to come off with a broken arm.* Mind you I reckon most of the trouble's caused by these Wanderers and Athletic Supporters. We've always known how to behave up here. *I wish you could see what they've done to the old ground. It's like that camp the Krauts put me in in* 42. Comes of joining that bloody market, I dare say. It's all beyond me. Still it's not a bad old life really and at least the beer tastes like beer since they stopped fetching it up from London in tin cans!

Chapter 17

Whitey spent the next twenty four hours in the studio. King's party had come well prepared with provisions and blankets and he even got some sleep.

The swarthy man, he discovered, had made no attempt to take over the control room single-handed, but had shot the internal Strikers, summoned the two outside men, killed them also, then admitted King and his party. Stan Linley had refused to cooperate, but his was the only resistance from the technical staff. The other bodies on the landing belonged to those Strikers who had come to investigate and to some norms seeking an escape route from the terror below.

It had taken five or so hours for the fighting in and around Wembley to die down and since that time the studio had been used as the control centre for the Jays' London operations.

"It's a case of keeping things stirred up," King explained happily. "The real fighting's going on along the border areas. But this is where the power is, here in London. We've got to pick our moment to produce Sheldrake out of the hat. It's no use just creating a new leader by force, he's got to have the support of the people too."

"The people you are helping to kill off so that

they will love Sheldrake," said Whitey.

"Stop being so reffing naive."

"And the Americans? What's in this for them?"

"Less than they think," said King with a confident smile. "They're not doing much anyway. Providing weapons, that's about the strength of it. It's pure self interest. They want to keep a finger-hold on Europe. Every continental country has given them the brown eye in the past ten years. So they want to create a bit of goodwill with us and also, of course, to prevent the kind of rapprochement with the E.E.C. the Directors were planning."

"Shooting that helicopter down must have helped them there," commented Whitey.

"Yes," said King thoughtfully. "Yes, it must."

As far as Whitey could ascertain, Hydrangea was safe. He hoped she was staying behind the sophisticated defenses of the American Embassy and not still going on with her spy-role as Chaucer's assistant.

During the afternoon of the day after the Wembley disaster, things became very quiet and King grew more and more restless. He tried to contact Sheldrake by radio-telephone several times and finally established that he had been touring the border areas but was returning to London that evening.

"Let's go," said King.

"Who? Me?" asked Whitey.

"Please yourself. You want to stay here, you stay here."

"No, no. I'll come. Where are we going?"

"To see Sheldrake."

"At Athletic House?"

King looked at him with a wry grin.

"Not yet awhile," he said. "Things don't just change over night. Look at the job they had to do on you. Me, I'm still high on the relegation list at A.H."

"Where then?"

"The Embassy," said King. "Nice neutral spot. It's quite reasonable that Sheldrake should go there for talks and it's well out of the way of any curious eyes."

The thought of going to the Embassy and possibly seeing Hydrangea gave Whitey the first pleasurable feelings he had experienced for twenty four hours. He focussed on the prospect as they left the stadium, keeping his mind and his eyes averted from the sprawl of human bodies which littered the roads. There were so many in the environs of Wembley that it was impossible to travel by car and for the first couple of miles they moved cautiously on foot.

There were many signs of looting both from shops and houses, and at one corner they came across three men searching bodies for valuables. Two of them fled at their approach but the third merely looked up from his grisly work, brandished a handful of money and said with a grin, "Plenty for all."

King shot him. Whitey looked at him, amazed.

"Why did you do that?" he demanded.

266

"He degrades us all," answered the young man, his features set in revulsion.

They proceeded in silence and a few streets further on, picked up an abandoned car, its bodywork battered and windscreen smashed, but still in working order.

A new horror became apparent as they approached central London. There was less evidence of street fighting here and though the shops offered much richer pickings, their more sophisticated security systems had for the most part protected them from looters. But in the last quarter mile of the Edgware Road Whitey saw at least two dozen victims of formal yussing, mostly hanging from lamp-posts or windows, and a line of condemned men had been bound to the railings round Hyde Park and shot.

"Who's been doing this?" he demanded.

"Our lads most likely," replied King. "They'll all be Association men."

"But why do it like this?"

"It's the agreed plan where there's time. Gives the business an air of formality. People will find it more reassuring in the long run than mere assassination. It's purposeful, makes you wonder what the fellow hanging there did to deserve execution."

Whitey regarded his young companion with revulsion. He looked quite serious. Suddenly his New York apartment, his liberal, concerned American friends, his stable, well-rewarded and meaningful life as a respected writer, seemed to be drifting beyond recall.

"No," he said emphatically.

"No what?" enquired King.

"Nothing."

No, I will not let it go. No, I will not accept what I am seeing here. Another five minutes brings me to the Embassy. Hydrangea. Safety. It may mean staying there for a few days, weeks even, till things calm down. Then out. Back to the States, back to my writing, with what a tale to tell. Exsmith must bear some of the blame. What a fool to think you can arm terrorists and exercise any control over them! His career might finish here, but he seemed a man of probity. He too would wish to do his best to put matters right. Whatever that entailed.

One thing was certain. Matters as they were at present were far from right.

At the Embassy gates they were taken out of the car and made to stand facing a blank wall till a check was made inside the building. It took long enough for Whitey to begin to worry, then they were ushered inside.

The first person he saw was Hydrangea.

"Thank God," she said with a depth of sincerity which caught at his heart. He found himself unable to answer and held her close without speech.

"Whitey. King. Glad you're OK," said Exsmith coming forward now with a broad smile on his face. Whitey disengaged himself from Hydrangea.

"Ambassador," he said, "do you know what's going on out there?"

"Well, my men radio in hourly reports," answered Exsmith. "Everything seems to be moving along smoothly. Wouldn't you say so, King?"

"Whitey is a little concerned that my men may have overstepped their brief," said King.

"Just how much of all this did you know in advance?" demanded Whitey. "Did you know that thousands of people were going to be killed? Did you know that men were going to be executed on the streets?"

"I'm merely giving what assistance I can to a worthwhile cause," answered Exsmith. "You wanted to stop the Association too, Whitey. We must allow Mr King to be judge of the best methods."

"You blind reffing fool!" shouted Whitey. "Can't you see the Jays are just using you?"

There was an interruption before Exsmith could reply. Hort, Hydrangea's hi-jack companion, came in and murmured something to the Ambassador.

"Bring them in," Exsmith answered. "Gentlemen, I have a surprise."

Through the door stepped Chaucer and Wildthorpe with a small band of Embassy guards in close attendance. The men were both very much the worse for wear. Wildthorpe in particular looked very grey. A streak of blood ran down his face from a cut across the brow and his clothes were torn and dishevelled.

269

"They were recognized in the street," explained Hort. "They just made it here about twenty yards ahead of a mob."

"Seeking sanctuary!" exclaimed Exsmith. "Touching. Well, gents, I think you know all these here assembled."

The two men did not reply but Whitey saw on their faces puzzlement modulate to concern as they tried to work out the significance of the grouping they saw before them. Chaucer solved it first and, typically, did not beat about the bush.

"I should have known," he said to Hydrangea. "From the start I should have known."

"She's an American citizen," urged Wildthorpe, still clinging to some faint hope that all was not as it seemed. "Why shouldn't she be here?"

"Forget it," said Chaucer wearily. "You as well, Singleton. It adds up. And as for trusting smelly little wankers like you, King, we must have been mad."

He jumped forward wildly swinging his fists at King who easily evaded the blows. A guard struck him lightly on the base of his neck and he half collapsed.

"You're too violent," said Exsmith. "Guards, take him out. Give him back to the crowd."

"Both of them, sir?"

"Just this one. The other we'll keep a little longer."

Chaucer was dragged past the now ashen-faced

Wildthorpe to the door. Here he recovered sufficiently to speak.

"For God's sake!" he cried, looking wildly round the room. His gaze fell on Whitey. "Whitey! Twice I helped you. I could have had you killed. You too, girl. Don't let them do this!"

Hydrangea stepped forward before Whitey could answer. Her voice was low, controlled.

"I still remember what you did in that prison cell. I've had to pretend it was forgotten, but it wasn't. Never. Does that answer you?"

"But you love me. You told me you loved me," said Chaucer desperately. "That's why I had him yussed as a glib. For you. Whitey . . ."

The guards tugged harder and Chaucer was dragged through the door. His voice cut off suddenly. Whitey tried desperately to find words but they would not come.

"They'll tear him to pieces," said Wildthorpe. He staggered a little and looked ready to collapse.

"Have a seat, sir," said Exsmith, concerned.

"We needn't bother to chuck this one out," said King contemptuously. "Just shout 'boo!' and he'll drop dead."

Wildthorpe turned his bowed head slightly to look at Whitey, but did not speak. Exsmith was fussing round him, offering a large glass of brandy. Whitey turned away, finding this solicitude grotesque and distasteful, and concentrated his attention on Hydrangea.

"You were his mistress," he said evenly.

"I should have thought it was obvious. He

271

wasn't just going to trust me for no reason." She spoke defiantly, but looked at him with concern in her eyes.

"Yes, obvious," he murmured. "Forget it. Does Exsmith know what he's got himself into here?"

"I think so," she said. "God, Whitey, I was worried about you. I wanted to go to Wembley with Chaucer, just to be near you, but they wouldn't let me."

"I'm touched. So you knew what was going to happen?"

"Not precisely, no," she answered, evading his gaze. "Look, Whitey, it's for the best."

"I've been a fool," he said bitterly. "I should have known the Jays would have tried for a take-over. But I thought the Embassy would have kept some kind of control."

He turned from Hydrangea and, uninvited, helped himself to a drink. Wildthorpe was looking slightly more healthy now and King was walking impatiently round the polished table in the centre of the large reception room.

"Where the hell's Sheldrake?" he demanded.

On cue, the door opened and Sheldrake entered. He stopped short at the sight of Wildthorpe.

"What's he doing here?" he demanded, but did not wait for an answer. "There's a crowd outside. They've got hold of Chaucer somehow. The poor reffer; what they're doing to him, it turned my guts."

272

"Oh dear," said Exsmith. "He was here, but he left."

"What's the news?" demanded King.

"It's going well. With a lot of help from our boys, things have been really humming. I reckon it's time to come out in the open."

"Fine," said King. "We'll coordinate from Wembley, get a nation-wide tele-cast. You in the middle of the pitch, perhaps. What a setting!"

"But don't fool yourself," said Sheldrake warningly. "There's a lot of fight left in those Strikers. Things will really explode once the broadcast goes out. They're not all going to lay down their arms just on my say so."

"That's OK. We're ready," said King confidently.

"Not quite," said Sheldrake. "Exsmith?"

He looked around for the Ambassador who had self-effacingly retired to a corner by the large marble fireplace. Can't he see that he's being treated like the hired help? wondered Whitey.

"Yes?" said Exsmith.

"There's been a cock-up with some of our units," said Sheldrake. "A lot of that ammo we had from you turned out to be for the old PF 70's, not the new 72's we've got. Has the new delivery you promised arrived yet?"

"Oh yes," said Exsmith, like a shopkeeper re-assuring an impatient customer. "It's all here, ready for distribution."

"Fine," said Sheldrake. "I've brought my quarter-master with me. I'll leave him to make arrangements. Now, there are one or two other matters King and I had better talk over while we're here. Would you mind leaving us alone?"

This ultimate arrogance surely must make Exsmith explode, thought Whitey, but the Ambassador looked unmoved.

"Of course," he said. "Certainly. Anything you wish. Gentlemen. Lady."

He began ushering Whitey, Wildthorpe and Hydrangea to the door.

"Just one thing," said King. "What's going to happen to him?"

He nodded at Wildthorpe.

"You afraid of me or something, son?" asked the old Director.

"No. Not any longer. You're finished now," said King calmly.

"Back in '79 we were three goals down at half-time at Wembley," said Wildthorpe. "They said we were finished then. But we took the Cup back up the Ml the next day."

"I remember that," said Whitey. "It was one of the saddest days of my life."

"You're getting your halves mixed up, old man," said King. "Half-time's long past. The next whistle is the last. You should have died at Wembley."

"Aye," said Wildthorpe. "Plenty did."

"Which reminds me," interjected Sheldrake. "What the hell happened to that chopper? That was a bad business killing all those Euros like that. We can't afford any continental interference at the moment."

"A mistake," said King. "No-one's admitting anything. We'll try to blame the Association."

"It's all right," said Exsmith assuringly, "there's no danger from the Continent. My government has assured all interested countries that we are keeping a watchdog eye on the situation here and will help press any claims for reparation when things return to normal."

"You've done *what?*" demanded Sheldrake furiously. "For Christ's sake, I thought you wanted to keep in the background? What the hell do you mean by going around giving assurances for someone else's country?"

"Please, please! Don't be offended. Of course any open interference in this country's internal affairs would be quite unwarranted. Unless, of course, it were formally requested by the country's accredited representative."

"Wait a minute," said Sheldrake suddenly thoughtful. "That helicopter. You had it shot down, didn't you, Exsmith?"

"That's a thoroughly irresponsible accusation," rebuked Exsmith. But there was a smile on his face. "Why should I arrange such a thing?"

"I don't know. But I warn you, if your precious government wants to keep its links with England, you stick to what we arranged. All you've got to do at the moment is to see to it our units are kept supplied . . ."

His voice tailed away.

"The ammunition," said King.

Suddenly they were all very busy with their thoughts.

"How are you feeling now, Mr. Wildthorpe?" asked Exsmith.

"Much better, thanks," answered Wildthorpe who did indeed look very much improved. He shook off Exsmith's helping hand, stepped back a pace and spoke formally. "Mr. Ambassador, on behalf of the sovereign state of England in association with the northern and western territories known as Scotland and Wales, I would like to request and invite the assistance of the United States of America to stem our present civil unrest."

You've got to admire the old reffer's nerve, thought Whitey, hoping that the old man would at least receive a courteous answer.

Exsmith smiled blandly and glanced at his watch.

"I thought you'd never ask," he said. "Though, in strictest terms, you are about five minutes early. Gentlemen, the extra arms you requested are indeed being supplied. But with them we are supplying men to bear them. The first troopplanes should just be landing."

Hope chased bewilderment from Wildthorpe's face as the others tried to grasp what was happening.

"You bastard," said Sheldrake.

"I can't ignore a request for help," said Exsmith calmly.

"And if he hadn't asked?"

"Someone always asks," answered Exsmith. "Gentlemen, you are under arrest."

For the first time Whitey noticed Hort and Hydrangea had guns in their hands. Sheldrake and King looked at each other desperately.

"Don't," said Hort reasonably.

But Whitey could have told him that men who see what they have worked and schemed for suddenly being pulled away from under their noses move out of the realm of reason.

They broke, left and right. Sheldrake took Hort's bullet full in the chest but retained enough momentum to crash into his slayer and bear him to the ground.

King went lower, took Hydrangea's legs from under her while she fired harmlessly into the wall, rolled to his feet in the same movement and reached the door.

But Hydrangea recovered quickly too and, rolling over on her stomach, she brought up her gun to bear on King as he wrenched at the door-handle. It was impossible to miss.

"No!" shouted Whitey and stepped in between.

He too had moved beyond reason. What he was denying so emphatically he could not have explained. But it didn't seem to matter whether he was yelling 'No!' to King dying, or 'No!' to Hydrangea becoming a killer. Perhaps he was shouting 'No!' to all killing and all dying and all causes and creeds; and shouting it the louder because he knew somehow he would never shout it again.

Hydrangea fired. But she had hesitated and changed her aim and the bullet crashed high into the woodwork of the door, slamming it shut behind the fleeing youth.

"No sweat," said Exsmith calmly. "They'll get him downstairs."

"I don't think so," said Whitey, helping Hydrangea to her feet. "He takes a lot of getting. Thanks for not shooting me, by the way."

"Perhaps I should have," said Hydrangea.

Whitey was right. King disappeared without trace, but it was too late for him to use the information he had acquired. Within twenty-four hours, American troops had taken control of all the large towns. Within forty-eight hours the Jays were being attacked in their most secret hideouts. American Intelligence had been very efficient in the last few weeks. And within seventy-two hours almost the only gunfire to be heard was the short economical bursts with which Jay prisoners were executed.

All this time Whitey stayed within the Embassy, neither a prisoner nor a free man. He stayed because he did not know where to go or what to do if he left.

Hydrangea came to him the first night, but after that no more.

They had talked; or rather he had asked questions, demanded answers, ignoring her attempts to urge him to love-making.

"This was all planned?"

"Yes."

"You knew it?"

"Some of it."

"And when it's all over, what then?"

"Peace, I guess."

"But the Americans stay?"

"Well, not all the troops, you understand. Of course not."

"But they stay? The government doesn't govern without their say so? Laws aren't passed, changes made, monies spent, without some rubber stamp from Washington?"

"Well, yes, yes, I suppose so. For a while. But there will *be* laws. Isn't that better than what has been here? Isn't any stable government better than anarchy?"

"I don't know," he answered, turning from her. "I don't know."

She rose and left. They had not mentioned Chaucer.

He didn't see Exsmith for nearly a week, then he was summoned to his office. Present also were two middle-aged sober-suited men.

"Come in, Whitey," said Exsmith. "Pleased to see you. May I introduce Mr. Hain and Mr. Carradoc, two of our government advisers who've been posted to England to help with the rehabilitation programme. Now, the thing is, Whitey, how do you see your future?"

"Future?"

"Yeah. You must have been giving it a lot of thought. These are stirring times for this little island. Everyone's full of hopes and uncertainties. I'm sure you're no different. What do you want to do with yourself."

"I'm not sure. Write again, I guess. Not straightaway, perhaps, but soon. Yes, that's it, on balance. I should like to go back to the States, rest up for a while, then get back to work."

As he spoke, the words suddenly became true. This was what he really did want to do. Get out of this town, this country. Go where there was space and sunshine, and new memories waited to be formed to bring balance and shape to the old. Then write. Not articles this time. Not paper pellets to flick and irritate for a few seconds. But a book, documentary, history, fiction, he wasn't sure which. But it would contain all this.

Exsmith was speaking again, sympathetically but firmly.

"I'm afraid that won't be possible, Whitey. Not for a while. No, you see, the thing is, our government thinks it best that entry visas to citizens of this country be restricted only to accredited diplomatic and trade representatives for a while. In any case, your own country has decided to place similar limitations on exit permits."

"Hold hard!" said Whitey. "You forget, I'm an American citizen and have been for several years."

"I'm afraid not," said Exsmith. "Don't you recall, you renounced your citizenship both by written and oral declaration only a few weeks ago? I'm afraid the machinery went into motion and your name's been removed."

"But you know why I did that, you know I had to . . ."

He stopped. Of course they knew. It wasn't a negotiable point.

"Can I reapply?"

"Perhaps. Later perhaps. But meanwhile, what about work?"

The man called Hain spoke for the first time.

"Mr. Singleton," he said, "this country needs men like you at the moment. You've been working for Mr. Wildthorpe recently, I believe, in the field of public relations. This is my special interest and this is what I'm here to advise on. We can use you in a variety of interesting and meaningful projects that your government has in hand."

"Propaganda, you mean," said Whitey.

"I prefer public relations, but use what term you will. It's a worthwhile job with a big future."

"Thanks. I'll think about it. But I feel I may prefer to make my own arrangements."

"That's your privilege, Whitey," said Exsmith. "But before you go, Mr. Carradoc would like to say a few words."

"I'm attached to the Justice Department," said Carradoc in a rapid monotonous voice. "Until such time as the system can be reviewed and overhauled, it is arguable that the laws under which the old system operated must be, de facto, the basis of jurisprudence in this country. Mr. Singleton, you are a convicted criminal enjoying at the moment a term of parole. No, let me finish, that's what it amounts to. One of the conditions of this parole refers specially to your employment, and it is arguable that for you to abandon or refuse to return to this employment, or some similar employment of an acceptable nature, would constitute a breach of parole."

"You stinking bastards," said Whitey slowly.

"Whitey! Please! We're trying to help. You and your country both. Look, you can do well. Think what the future can hold for you. Miss Chesterman, Hydrangea you call her, she's very fond of you, I know that. You might want to marry, bring up a family. I promise you your children would be entitled to dual citizenship. And it's in your power to make sure there's a safe and stable environment for them to grow up in. The alternative . . . well, hell, who wants to talk about that? What do you say?"

"I'll think about it," said Whitey, rising.

"Be quick," said Exsmith. Whitey did not reply, but left the room.

In the outer office stood Hydrangea. She looked at him hopefully, an unspoken question in her eyes.

"I told them I'd think about it," said Whitey walking past her and out of the room.

Nixon Lectures : Fifth Series

Conclusion of final lecture

You have listened to me patiently during these last few weeks and I have tried to reward your patience with an objective picture of the state of Britain in this modern age.

But you will appreciate how hard it is for me to remain purely objective as I describe the horrors which the Four Clubs have brought to my old country. I still share in those horrors, though I have left them behind for ever. Every time I sign my name, I am reminded of them. My friends often ask me why I am called 'Whitey'. It's nothing to do with my colouring, I assure you. The truth of the matter is that my father was a great football fan and the team he loved most of all played at a ground called White Hart Lane. He would have named me after the whole team, but my mother protested, so he contented himself with having a son called White Hart Singleton. He was a fine man. He died in the great Birmingham riot of 1982. I was the only survivor from those two coachloads of fans.

Well, so much for my name. I have never been to the ground since that day and I do not think I shall ever go back again. For while terrorism, and the rule of the mob, and the law of the strongest prevail in Britain, I cannot return. Let us pray that there are a few Britons still left who can remain untarnished by what is going on around them. Let us thank God that this great country which has adopted me still has a footing on British soil and may still be an influence for a return to traditional morality and the rule of law. Human relationships lie at the bottom of both these. If we are true to those who love us, we have laid the basis of the great society.

Thank you for your patience. Tomorrow I leave for Tokyo and after that I shall visit the Sudan. I assure you an African war holds no fears for a man who has faced such a distinguished audience as this! But as always I shall look forward eagerly to returning to the last and greatest stronghold of freedom in the modern world. Thank you for letting me in.

Chapter 18

It was a glorious late February day, containing all the promise of Spring. Hydrangea had put the pram out in the sunshine for the first time ever and kept on going into the garden to make sure all was well.

After lunch when Whitey rose from his chair and put his jacket on, she asked, "Are you going to the match?"

"Yes. Why?"

"I thought it was such a lovely day, we might go out for a little run somewhere. What about it?"

Whitey hesitated, then shook his head.

"Tomorrow, eh? If the weather holds. I've been looking forward to today's game. It's the first time for two months the ground will be fit to play decent football on."

Hydrangea made a moue of disappointment then grinned.

"OK. But tomorrow, we go. Even if it snows. Take your overcoat now, this sunshine can be deceptive."

At the end of the street the policeman who was permanently there since the last car-bomb saluted him.

"Morning Mr. Singleton."

"Morning, Joe. Bet you wish you were on football duty."

"You can say that again."

Whitey walked on, thinking that his father would have found the policeman reassuringly familiar thirty years ago. Except for the machine-pistol he carried in the crook of his arm.

The streets became progressively busier as he approached the ground. Getting football going again had been one of the brainwaves emanating from Whitey's own department. It had taken a little while to get things under way, but the teams were now over half-way through their first full season, and as league and cup hopes became more and more clarified, so interest had grown, till the better games had become sell-outs.

The theory was that old Four Club loyalties could most easily be dissipated in this way, and it seemed to be working. Of course, stringent methods of dealing with rowdyism, both on and off the field, had been introduced from the start. No-one wanted to risk the development of the early eighties situation which had led to the Four Clubs.

Everyone looked happy today. The sunshine and anticipation of a good match had warmed their spirits, continuing the job begun by the recent relaxation of tax controls as the economy began to move upwards. Whitey knew the controls could have been slackened even further, but prosperity brought its own dangers. Gratitude was only shortlived. Today's gratefully accepted gift quickly became tomorrow's automatic expectation. Besides, while an American presence in Europe was sufficient reward for the politicians, the businessmen who had pumped millions of dollars into England were now looking for a return on their investment.

Still, it was good to be walking along Tottenham High Road once more, with the floodlights of White Hart Lane visible in the distance.

He had a season ticket for the main stand, but he rarely used it, preferring to pass through the turnstile on to the terraces. When asked about this he always answered, "My dad used to say you start watching football when you can't play it, and you start sitting down to watch when you can't stand."

There were still fifty minutes to kick-off time but already the terraces were almost full. He bought a programme and made his way up the terracing to the very top, where he halted and surveyed the pitch. It looked in good health from up here, green and lush in the sunlight.

His programme listed the teams as expected. It was surprising how in both sides there were two or three names surviving from the pre-dissolution days. Youngsters then, their chosen careers nipped in the bud, now they returned as elder statesmen to bring expertise and stability to a generation who had grown up with little formal experience of the game.

The programme also told him that the guest of honour that day was going to be Sam Exsmith, the American Ambassador. And the most important man in the country, added Whitey mentally. It was a current Whitehall joke that the second most important man in the country was Premier Wildthorpe if you didn't count Exsmith's dog.

A young man with a drooping blond moustache shouldered his way up the terracing and came to a halt beside Whitey.

"Lovely day for it," he said cheerfully.

"It is," agreed Whitey.

"Any team changes?"

"Have a look," said Whitey, handing over his programme. The young man scanned it briefly and returned it.

"Ta," he said slipping into his pocket the sheet of paper he had taken from between the programme pages.

Down below a band had appeared on the pitch and now they struck up 'When The Saints Go Marching In.' Soon the fans on the terraces were singing lustily. It was curious, Whitey had observed, that they were much more responsive to musical accompaniment than they had been in the seventies when bands were frequently inaudible through the rival tunes being chanted round the ground.

"That moustache looks terrible," he said under cover of the noise.

"Rest assured. Underneath it I'm as bare-faced as ever," answered King. "How's Hydrangea?"

"Fine. Another year and she'll be back at work. She misses it, I think."

"That's good. It was a useful contact. She never suspects anything?"

"No," said Whitey sadly. "Women think that a leopard could change its spots for love. By the way, I wish you'd be more careful where you're putting those cars. My greenhouse was ruined by the last blast."

"You shouldn't live so close to the Commissioner of Police. That reminds me. You drive here today?"

"No."

"Good. Well, don't stray near the car-park afterwards."

"What? You're trying for Exsmith again?"

King shrugged.

"Why not? It keeps the interest going. Like the band, till the big game starts."

"I suppose so."

They joined in the singing now, till the band stopped and the players ran out on the field, forming two lines for the presentation ceremony.

Out of the tunnel marched the official party. In the centre of the group, Whitey could just make out Exsmith. The man's courage had to be admired. Even with his bullet-proof waistcoat and his four body-guards constantly moving around to keep their bodies between Exsmith and possible sources of attack, he was still very vulnerable.

The band struck up the American anthem. In the main stand, they began to sing, but here upon the terraces few mouths opened.

Then suddenly a voice was raised in a distant corner, a strong tenor which sent one word floating over the ground. Immediately there were waves of violent movement in the crowd as men began to converge on the singer. These were policemen too, Whitey told himself, but not such as his father would have recognized thirty years ago.

Now the word was sung out again from another part of the ground. Movement again, but this time the word was taken up elsewhere immediately and the waves became uncertain, erratic, till finally they died away completely as from all corners the word was sounded out till the band was drowned fathoms deep in the noise.

ALBION! ALBION! ALBION!

Beside him, King had joined in, his eyes shining, his absurd moustache looking in danger of being blown off by the force of his voice.

Whitey looked at him affectionately. He was still young enough to hope.

But even, perhaps especially, when the future looked black beyond redemption, a man needed something to give himself to.

Muted at first, but with increasing power, he joined in the chant.

The employees of G.K. Hall hope you have enjoyed this Large Print book. All our Large Print titles are designed for easy reading, and all our books are made to last. Other G.K. Hall books are available at your library, through selected bookstores, or directly from us.

For information about titles, please call:

(800) 223-2336

To share your comments, please write:

Publisher
G.K. Hall & Co.
P.O. Box 159
Thorndike, ME 04986